FATAL DEBT

DOROTHY HOWELL

FATAL DEBT

Copyright © 2013 Dorothy Howell

Cover Design by Evie Cook
Edited by William F. Wu
Formatted by IRONHORSE Formatting

ISBN-13: 978-0-9856930-1-5

With love to Stacy, Judy, Seth, Brian, and David

The author is eternally grateful to everyone who generously gave their time, effort, and support to the creation of this book. Some of them are: Judith Branstetter, Stacy Howell, David Howell, William F. Wu, Ph.D., Evie Cook, Kristina Minutella, Web Crafters Design, and Ironhorse Formatting.

CHAPTER ONE

"Repo the Sullivans's TV," Manny said, gesturing to the print-out on his desk.

"What? The Sullivans? No way," I told him.

"Today," he said. "They're too far past due. We can't carry them."

"Come on, Manny, not the Sullivans," I said. "They're nice people. They've had an account with us for twenty years, or something. I can't repossess their television."

Manny Franco who, technically, was my supervisor—though I disagreed with the disparity in our positions on many levels—lowered himself into his chair and dug his heels into the carpet to roll himself up to his desk.

"We never should have made that loan. They can't afford it," he said, swiping his damp forehead with his palm.

Manny was always stressed. He was only an inch taller than me—and at five-feet, nine-inches I'm tall for a girl—and outweighed me by at least a hundred pounds. He wore his black hair long and slicked back in waves. His suits always looked a little rumpled and his collar a size too small.

I was sitting in the chair beside Manny's desk in the office of Mid-America Financial Services, a nationwide consumer finance company that granted personal loans, second mortgages, and did some dealer financing for things like TVs, stereos, and furniture.

I'd worked all sorts of jobs in the past few years. Data entry, waitressing, sales clerk, then a good job as an admin assistant for a major corporation that went under, taking me with it. Piercing ears at the mall landed me the job at Mid-America.

Something about snapping on latex gloves and driving a metal spike

1

through the flesh of infants and children had impressed Mr. Burrows, the branch manager, and he'd hired me several months ago as an asset manager.

While that might sound like a fabulous job—that came with a fabulous salary—not so. But the big three-oh was on the horizon, I'd been unemployed *forever*, and I was still working on my B.A., so I didn't have a lot of options. Like many other people in the country, I'd been desperate for a paycheck. Besides, I hadn't decided what my future held—beyond taking over the world, the only thing I knew for sure I wanted to do with my life.

I liked justice. I liked the scales to balance, which was one of the things that appealed to me about my job with Mid-America. It gave me a chance to be judge, jury, and executioner, at times, to mete out a little justice for my customer's benefit and, sometimes, for Mid-America's benefit.

I didn't like it when things didn't even out.

According to Mid-America, the position of asset manager required that I telephoned customers who were behind on their payments and work with them to get their accounts up to date. I was okay with helping people get back on their feet, financially—I remember well the Summer of Spam, as I thought of it, when I was ten years old and my dad lost his job.

I was also expected to take whatever steps were necessary to collect Mid-America's accounts, including pursuing legal action and repossessing collateral.No way was I doing that, so I put my own twist on the position.

"The Sullivans are doing okay," I said to Manny, even though I knew they weren't. But I liked them, two sweet old people, both in their sixties.

"Repo the TV, Dana," Manny said.

"Mr. Sullivan lost his part-time job," I said.

Manny was unmoved. He'd heard this story a zillion times.

"He has another job lined up," I said, even though I knew it wasn't true. "They'll have the money soon."

Manny's gaze narrowed, studying me, like he thought maybe I was just shining him on—which I was. But I'm as good at the stare-down as anybody so I gazed right back at Manny without blinking an eye.

"I have to answer to Corporate on this," he said.

Corporate. What a bunch of jackasses.

"Pick up the TV, Dana. Now," Manny said, then turned to his computer.I gathered my stuff and left the office with one thought burning in my mind: how the heck was I going to get out of repoing the

Sullivans' television and still keep my job?

* * *

I fumed as I drove out of Mid-America's parking lot and headed for the freeway. Luckily, I had on a favorite pants and jacket outfit, the sun shone bright, and I was treated to a gorgeous late October day here in Santa Flores.

The city was, admittedly, not one of Southern California's finest, even though it was situated half-way between Los Angeles and Palm Springs, at the base of the mountains leading up to the Big Bear and Lake Arrowhead ski resorts. But don't let that prestigious location give you any ideas. A few years back Santa Flores was dubbed the Murder Capital of America.

Yes, the Murder Capital of America was my home. A place where you could get killed for your shoes. I'd lived there all my life. My whole family lived there too, except my older brother who'd married and moved up north about a year ago; Mom's still giving him "another month or so" before she's sure he'll move back.

Like a lot of other places, things had gone badly for Santa Flores in the last few decades. The steel mill shut down, the railroad yard moved, the Air Force base closed. Gangs moved in from L.A. The real estate bubble burst. Businesses closed. The only thing on the upswing was the number of people out of work.

I took the 215 freeway north and exited on State Street—the Sullivans had been behind on their account so many times I knew the way to their house without my GPS—then made my way to Devon, a nice area—once—but that was before I was born. Gangs had brought drugs and violence. Some of the houses were abandoned, long ago falling to ruin. A few families valiantly kept up their yards and painted over the graffiti on their fences; most just hung on.

As I parked outside the chain link fence that surrounded the Sullivans' little stucco home, I noted the place needed painting. The grass was dead. Old lawn chairs and broken flower pots were overturned beside the porch.

Despite everything, Arthur and Gladys Sullivan were sweet, loveable old people, the kind you couldn't say no to—though Mid-America should have said "no" to their last loan request. They were on a fixed income; their budget was tight. They'd needed five hundred dollars to fix their car, and Mr. Sullivan needed that car to get to his part-time job.

3

Mid-America had approved the loan, picking up their 42-inch Sony television for collateral.

They'd fallen behind on their payments a few months ago but I'd let it go—thus, the *twist* I'd put on my job description—giving them time to get some money together. Now Manny—and Corporate—thought I'd held off too long. I had, but that didn't mean I was going to take their TV.

I got out of my Honda. The front gate squeaked when I opened it, the boards of the porch groaned, the screen door rattled. I knocked, hoping the Sullivans wouldn't be there. They were.

Mr. Sullivan opened the door also squeaking, groaning, and rattling. His file indicated he was 67. He looked older. His hair appeared more white than gray against his black skin. He wore denim jeans and a red flannel shirt buttoned at the collar; he walked on the backs of his corduroy house slippers.

He squinted at me and smiled, showing a missing bottom tooth, then turned back inside.

"Look who's here," he called. "It's that Mid-America girl."

I'm here to repo his TV and he's glad to see me. Great.

"Dana Mackenzie," I said, reminding him of my name.

He led the way into the living room. The house was neat and clean, decorated with lace doilies and pictures of Jesus. It smelled like boiling beans and linoleum.

Mrs. Sullivan sat on a worn sofa wearing a floral house coat with snaps up the front. She was watching television, of course.

"Hi, Mrs. Sullivan," I said.

She glanced up at me. "Hi, honey."

"Mama's watching her stories," Mr. Sullivan said.

A soap opera, I realized, glancing at the screen.

Mr. Sullivan eased onto his threadbare recliner and I sat in a straight-backed chair beside him. We exchanged pleasantries and I stalled, but finally came to the point.

"I'm sorry, Mr. Sullivan, but my boss reviewed your account, and he wants me to pick up your television," I said.

He just looked at me, taking it in, making me feel worse, then shook his head.

"Well, if you got to, you got to." He looked over at his wife. "But how's Mama gonna watch her stories? She loves her stories. What's she gonna do?"

He wasn't so much asking me as musing aloud how he'd let her down.

If ever I'd been tempted to give a customer some money, this was it.

They were old people. They didn't have much. The home they'd bought when they were young was decaying. The neighborhood they'd invested their time and emotion in had fallen to criminals. Their health was about gone. Not much was left for them—except Mrs. Sullivan's stories, and Mr. Sullivan's ability to let her watch them.

I'd be fired on the spot if I made a payment on a customer's account. A partial payment, a few cents, it wouldn't matter. Even if I loaned it to them, I'd be gone. And I couldn't afford to lose my job.

"We don't get money again until the first of the month," Mr. Sullivan said. "I've got Mama's medicine money. I could give you that."

I cringed.

"I'll call Leonard," I said.

Leonard was their grandson. He'd had an account with Mid-America some time back. Lots of families had accounts with us. It wasn't unusual. They passed us around and talked about us over holiday meals.

Leonard was about my age. He had trouble holding a job—not finding a job, like most people, just holding onto it. He'd been late on his payments more times than not, yet there was something very likeable about him. I had no problem calling him and asking for money on his grandparents' behalf.

"He's a good boy," Mr. Sullivan said. "We raised him, me and Mama, after his daddy died and his mama took off. He's got a new job. I'll call him. He'll help us out."

I felt more relieved than Mr. Sullivan appeared.

"I'll tell him to come by the house after he gets off work," Mr. Sullivan said. "Maybe he can drive me down to your office."

I didn't want to take the chance that something might come up, so I said, "I'll come back out and pick up the money."

"You come on back at supper time," Mr. Sullivan said.

I waved to Mrs. Sullivan, who didn't seem to notice, thanked Mr. Sullivan, and left.

* * *

In the short time I'd worked for Mid-America, the company had been bought out by a major conglomerate, then a mega-conglomerate, neither of which had done much except cause everyone a lot of unnecessary headaches.

Our office was located in downtown Santa Flores in a two-story building on Fifth Street. Just down the block were the post office, the courthouse, and all sorts of restaurants, bars, and office buildings.

Mid-America had one of the offices on the ground floor that offered great "signage," according to a guy in a thousand-dollar-suit who'd come out from the corporate office in Chicago to evaluate our location and formulate an enhanced marketing plan, and then had, apparently, forgotten we existed.

All I cared about was keeping our current location so I could look out our big plate glass window all day.

When I got back to the office Manny was more concerned with a possible foreclosure on a house out in Webster, a town about twenty minutes east of Santa Flores. He accepted my explanation of why I wasn't carrying a 42-inch Sony television with only a brief nod, and I got on with my work.

My desk sat at the rear of the office near Manny's. This placement was Corporate's decision, not mine. According to Mid-America's seating chart, the cashier who took payments from our walk-in customers sat at the counter up front. Just behind her were the two financial reps who handled the lending end of the business, along with Inez Marshall, their supervisor who was, thankfully, not in the office today. The beige furniture, walls, and carpet, and seascapes in plastic frames, were about as generic as an office could get.

The mail had been delivered while I was out, and I saw a neat stack of envelopes centered on my desk—Corporate had not bestowed upon us online bill-paying capability, despite our fabulous signage. I got to look at the mail before anyone in the branch because I was anxious to know which of my customers had paid. Getting money together to make a payment was tough for my customers. I didn't want to be calling them if their payment was at the cashier's desk waiting to be posted.

I'd just about reached the bottom of the stack when a familiar return address leaped off the envelope and smacked me between the eyes.

Nick Travis.

My breath caught and I felt a smile spread across my face. Oh, yeah, this was the boost I needed right now.

I'd known Nick Travis in high school. Everybody knew Nick Travis. Football team captain, student body president, gorgeous hottie. He'd dated my best friend, Katie Jo Miller, for a short while—a very short while—when Katie Jo and I were sophomores and Nick was in his senior year.

Nick got her pregnant, made her have an abortion, then dumped her and left town.

Imagine my surprise all these years later to find an account on Mid-America's books from Nick Travis. He'd financed a high-end television and sound system. I hadn't even known he'd moved back to Santa Flores.

When I'd seen Nick Travis's name on the computer screen that day—and after I got myself up off the floor—I accessed his file and proceeded to learn everything there was to know about the man who'd ruined my best friend's life.

The copy of his driver's license that the TV dealer had provided indicated Nick was six-three, two hundred twenty pounds, brown hair, blue eyes. He'd moved back to Santa Flores a few months before the application was taken. He had checking and savings accounts at a credit union, two Visas with small balances, a Chevy that was financed, and a mortgage payment.

The mortgage surprised me because according to the application, Nick was unmarried. He had no dependents and paid no child support or alimony.

The shocker was that Nick worked for the Santa Flores Police Department as a detective. I guess they're pretty desperate these days—especially here in the Murder Capital of America.

Katie Jo's abortion had been rough. Her parents had been supportive but they were disappointed in their little girl. There were religious issues.

She stayed home for a long time. She wouldn't return phone calls. She refused to talk to anyone, even to me, her best friend. She was never the same after that. Neither were her parents. Neither was I.

The only one unscathed was Nick Travis.

I logged onto my computer and pulled up his account. A lot of people waited until the last minute to make their payment, getting it in to us just before it was considered late. Nick Travis was one of those people. According to his due date, today was the last day he could make his payment and avoid a late charge.

I looked at the computer screen, looked at his payment, and thought about Katie Jo Miller.

I ripped Nick Travis's check into tiny pieces and dropped it into my trash can.

* * *

At 4:50 I pulled up Nick Travis's account on my computer and called his office.

"Travis," he barked, when he came on the line. He sounded as if he was just short of a bad mood. I was about to make his afternoon.

I identified myself with my sweetest voice.

"I'm calling because I was looking over your account and I noticed that today is the last day to avoid a late charge," I said, "and we haven't

7

received your payment yet."

Silence. The cold, hard kind.

"I made that payment," he finally said.

I pictured cartoon-steam coming out of his ears.

"Well, it hasn't come in yet," I said. "You can bring it in, if you want to avoid the late charge."

"You close in five minutes."

I gasped—an Academy Award winning gasp—and said, "You're right. Looks like you'll have to pay that late charge."

I hung up feeling pleased with myself, and pleased for Katie Jo, too.

At five o'clock on the dot Carmen Chavez, our cashier, locked the door and began to count her cash drawer. Carmen was a few years younger than me, but was already married with a small child.

I was about to take off for the Sullivan place when a face appeared through the glass on our front door.

Nick Travis.

My heart did a little flip-flop.

I recognized him because he'd been into the office on previous months to make his payment. He'd changed so much I'd never have recognized him from high school.

Nick was taller now, bulkier as men got after their teenage years. In high school he'd been drop-dead gorgeous; now there was a blunted, more angular look to his face. Square jaw, strong chin, straight nose. Still good looking, but in a more rugged way.

He had on gray trousers, a navy blue sport coat, and a tie that actually looked good together. I wondered if he had a woman dressing him.

I was pretty sure Nick had recognized me from high school when he'd come into the office a few months ago and I'd waited on him at the counter. I'd seen that flash of recognition in his face, but he hadn't said anything. Maybe he didn't like being reminded of high school—or Katie Jo Miller.

Or maybe he was just being a jerk.

I unlocked the door and peered at him, pretending I didn't know who he was.

"We're closed," I told him.

"You called me just now about my payment," he said.

I stared, still pretending.

"Nick Travis," he said.

"Oh, right. You're the one with the late payment," I said.

"I sent my payment," he told me. "In plenty of time."

"It was never received, obviously," I said. "You can make your payment, if you'd like. We'll post it tomorrow. You'll have that late charge by then."

He glared at me. "Fine."

I let him in and couldn't help but take a long look as he headed toward the counter. My heart did a little pitter-pat. To compensate, I stepped to the power position behind the counter.

"You might want to stop payment on that check you claim you sent," I said.

He pulled his checkbook from the pocket of his sport jacket and said, "That will cost me another twenty bucks on top of the late charge."

I gave him my too-bad-for-you shrug.

"This is the fourth time this has happened in the last five months," Nick said. He dashed off his check, then ripped it out of the book.

I made him stand there and hold it out for a few seconds before I took it.

My stomach felt a little queasy, but that was probably because I'd trashed his check this morning, though my I'm-feeling-guilty stomach roll was a little different from what I experienced at the moment.

Or maybe it was Nick. I always felt a little nervous when he came into the office, but that was because he was in law enforcement. Policemen always made me feel as if they knew everything I'd done wrong, like they could somehow see inside me and know about the lipstick I shoplifted from Wal-mart when I was fourteen.

"I need a receipt," Nick said.

Carmen was busy counting the day's payments so I wrote out a receipt. When I looked up again I caught him eyeing the office, using his police detective X-ray vision to check out my trash can, no doubt.

"Here," I said, distracting him with the receipt.

Nick tucked it inside his checkbook, then headed for the door. I followed. Once outside, he looked back and gave me a half grin.

Nick had a grin other men would have paid serious bucks for. The kind of grin that made women melt into their shoes. For a second, I got lost in that grin. I started to melt.

Katie Jo had reacted the same way. How many other women had, too?

I locked the door, shut down my computer and left the office.

* * *

The neighborhood seemed oddly quiet when I pulled up in front of the Sullivan house. No one was outside. No kids played in the yards. No music blared from the nearby houses, no dogs barked. The sun was going down, the light fading.

I got out of my car and climbed onto the porch. The front door stood open a few inches. I knocked and the door swung open a little more. A lamp burned in the living room and the television played softly; it sounded like a basketball game was on.

"Mr. Sullivan? Hello?" I called.

I figured I'd find him asleep in front of the TV so I stepped inside and leaned around the corner.

No one was there. I walked farther into the room. Movement off to my right, down the hallway, caught my attention a fraction of a second before a man barreled into me. He hit me on the right shoulder and knocked me backwards. I stumbled over something and sat down hard on my butt, my feet flying into the air, my head thumping on the side of the recliner. Stunned, I sat there for a second or two, then scrambled to my feet more mad than hurt.

"Hey!" I shouted. But I was talking to myself. The man was gone, the front door slammed shut.

I straightened my clothes, restoring some sort of personal dignity. A minute passed before it occurred to me that I still hadn't seen the Sullivans.

"Mr. Sullivan?" I called.

I crept down the hallway and peered into the first bedroom on the left.

Mr. Sullivan lay on the floor. Dead.

CHAPTER TWO

Everything I'd eaten that day bounced once and shot upward. I gulped it down and edged closer to Mr. Sullivan. He lay on his side facing me, a dark spot on the front of his shirt, a trickle of blood seeping onto the floor.

I panicked. I knelt and shook his shoulder.

"Mr. Sullivan!"

He didn't respond. Just lay there. Still, quiet, unmoving.

Some things in life you just know. No one has to tell you, you don't need any previous experience, you don't have to read it on the Internet. You just know.

And I knew Mr. Sullivan was dead.

My legs gave out. I plopped onto the floor. My head got light.

Different ideas skittered through my mind. Get help. Call 9-1-1. Probably a dozen things I should do.

But I couldn't seem to move. All I could do was sit there staring at Mr. Sullivan in his denim jeans, his corduroy slippers with the broken backs, and his flannel shirt with the big stain on the front.

Sound intruded. A siren. A squawking radio. Voices. Running feet.

Two uniformed policemen charged into the bedroom, guns drawn. They yelled at me. I couldn't hear them with my heart pounding in my ears.

While one of the officers kept his gun trained on me, the other holstered his weapon. He touched the arm of my blazer.

All right, I didn't know much about police investigations, but this hardly seemed the time to admire my jacket, even though it cost a small fortune.

"Blood," the officer said.

That word oozed into the confusion in my mind.

I looked down. Blood covered my fingers.

"Get on your feet," the officer with the gun said.

It took a few more seconds but I finally realized what they were saying. They thought I'd had something to do with Mr. Sullivan's death.

My brain refused to process this information. My life flashed before me. My heart thundered in my chest. My stomach squeezed into a knot.

And then Nick Travis walked into the room.

He did a double-take when he saw me, then waved at the uniforms to put away their guns.

Nick leaned down. "Are you hurt?"

I heard him but couldn't seem to make much sense out of his question.

"Are you hurt?" he asked again, louder this time.

I looked up at him, and asked, "Where's Mrs. Sullivan?"

We stayed like that for a second or two, him leaning down, me looking up, staring into each other's eyes, with the horrible possibility of where Mrs. Sullivan might be arcing between us.

Nick spoke to one of the uniforms who hurried out of the room, then knelt in front of me. He picked up my hand and looked at my bloody fingertips. I realized he thought the blood was mine. He looked closer, then evidently satisfied I wasn't injured, released my arm.

"Did you see who did this?" he asked, gesturing vaguely to Mr. Sullivan.

"I just got here," I said.

I couldn't seem to stop looking at Mr. Sullivan. Nick caught my chin and turned me to face him.

"What happened?" he asked.

I squinted my eyes closed for a second. "Somebody ran into me when I came into the house."

"What did he look like?" Nick demanded.

"I—I'm not sure," I said.

"Tall, short, white, Hispanic, old, young, male, female?"

The urgency in Nick's voice prodded me to think harder.

"A man. Tall. White, I think," I said. "I only caught a glimpse."

"What was he wearing?" Nick asked.

"A hoodie," I said. "Black, or maybe navy blue."

Nick repeated the description to the other uniform who hurried away, then turned back to me.

"Would you recognize him if you saw him again?" he asked.

Right now I wasn't sure I could pick my own mother out of a line-up.

"I didn't see his face, just the side of it, I think. I don't know." I looked at the blood on my fingers and felt lightheaded again.

Nick caught me under my arms and pulled me up. He hustled me out of the room. I tried to cooperate but my feet seemed to be on backwards. At the doorway I turned back for a final look at Mr. Sullivan. Nick pulled me down the hallway before I could see him that last time.

Nick took me to the kitchen sink. He stuck my hand under the faucet and doused it with dishwashing detergent. .

"Breathe," he said.

He washed away the blood, dragged a dishtowel over my hand, then yanked off my blazer and tossed it on the table. The room spun and I leaned against him. He pulled me out the back door and dumped me on the top step of the cement porch.

"Keep breathing," he said and sat down beside me. He caught the back of my neck and pushed my head between my knees.

"Stay here," Nick said, and went back into the house.

I kept breathing. Gradually my head cleared. Behind me, inside the house, I heard all sorts of commotion. More officials arriving, going about their duties. Probably a half dozen vehicles were out front by now, lights pulsing, drawing neighbors out of their homes to gawk, point, and speculate.

All because a sweet old man, whose only goal in life was to keep a 42-inch Sony television for his wife, was dead.

Sometimes life really sucked.

When I take over the world, I'm definitely changing that.

The sky got darker and the street lights came on. I didn't want to be there, but leaving meant I'd have to go through the house and my stomach rolled at the prospect. All sorts of people were out front. My car was likely blocked in.

It occurred to me that I'd been lucky that Nick had walked into Mr. Sullivan's bedroom. A detective who didn't know me might assume I'd been part of the murder, as the uniforms had.

I didn't like feeling grateful to Nick Travis for anything.

I sat there long enough that the shock wore off and I got cold. My blazer was in the kitchen, but no way did I ever want to see that thing again.

The back door opened and Nick sat down beside me. I couldn't help but notice he gave off some serious heat. Not that I'd consider snuggling closer, just enough to make me anxious to leave.

"Feeling better?" he asked.

I wasn't exactly glad to see him, yet it was comforting, something familiar in this foreign, horrifying setting.

"Did you find Mrs. Sullivan?" I asked. If that sweet old lady were dead too, I didn't know how I'd handle it.

"No sign of her," Nick said.

Well, thank God for that much, I thought.

"I'm leaving now," I said.

Nick frowned. "You're coming with me."

No way was I going anywhere but home.

Nick seemed to read my expression and said, "I need you to come to the station."

My fear spun up again, but for a different reason.

"Am I under arrest?" I asked.

"I'm not arresting you," Nick said. "Not yet, anyway."

I shot to my feet. "I didn't do anything."

Nick rose. "You need to give us a statement."

"Okay, look, here's my statement," I told him. "I got here, some jerk bowled me over, I found Mr. Sullivan, and that's it."

Frown lines appeared between Nick's brows. "Are you refusing to cooperate with law enforcement in a murder investigation?"

"I'm supposed to be considered innocent until proven guilty," I told him.

"Then coming down to the station shouldn't be a problem for you— unless you have something to hide." He switched on his cop X-ray vision and drilled me with it. "Are you hiding something?"

I cringed. He was going to get me down to that police station and I was going to spill my guts over everything I'd done wrong in my entire life. The lipstick I'd shoplifted at Wal-mart. The N'Sync CD I'd conveniently forgotten to return to Lizzie Blake in junior high. The algebra test I'd cheated on. Everything. Every tawdry, underhanded, deceitful thing I'd done in my whole life—including throwing his payment in the trash four out of the last five months.

I squared my shoulders and pushed my chin a little higher, and announced," Of course, I don't have anything to hide."

"Then, let's go," he said.

When we got to the front of the house Nick put me into one of Santa Flores's finest's patrol cars and told me he'd have somebody bring my car down to the station.

Nice, being escorted away from a crime scene and loaded into a police car.

I knew he'd done this on purpose.

* * *

I'd been to the police station on Seventh Street a couple of times to pick up police reports for things relating to Mid-America's customers, but never farther into the building than the front desk. I'd gotten the shakes just going that far. So sitting across a desk from Homicide Detective Nick Travis in a room full of other cops was a real joy.

Even this late in the evening the telephones rang. Detectives moved around. Papers shuffled, conversations hummed.

Nick rolled back the sleeves of his shirt. He'd taken off his sport coat. A gun rested in a shoulder holster under his left arm.

"Want some coffee?" he asked.

I didn't intend to be here long, so no need to get comfortable.

"How did you get to the Sullivan house so fast?" I asked.

Nick rifled through his desk drawers. "Neighbors heard shots fired, called it in. We were in the area on another call."

He made it sound routine.

"So that's how Mr. Sullivan…died?" I asked.

Nick stopped searching for whatever he'd been searching for and looked at me. His face softened, just a little.

"Yeah," he said. "He was shot. Two rounds in the chest. Point blank. He died instantly."

I don't know about that died-instantly thing. Seems to me that unless you passed away in your sleep you'd have those last few seconds when you knew your number had been called—or in the case of Mr. Sullivan, somebody had called it for you.

I didn't want to think about death anymore. I wanted this over and done with.

"What do you want to know?" I asked Nick.

He seemed to sense my mood change because he went back to searching through the drawers and came up with a pen and a form of some sort, and started filling it out.

"What were you doing out there?" he asked.

"Mr. Sullivan told me to come," I said. "He was behind on his account and I was going to pick up money from him."

Nick stopped writing. "You went out to that neighborhood by yourself, at that time of night?"

I shrugged. "Sure."

"That's a dangerous area. You shouldn't go out there."

"Thanks, Mom," I told him.

Nick glared at me for a few seconds, then went on to his next question.

"Was Sullivan giving you a large sum of money?" he asked.

I guess he thought robbery might have been a motive for Mr. Sullivan's shooting.

"Around a hundred bucks," I said. "Have you found Mrs. Sullivan yet?"

"We're trying to track her down," he said.

"Her sister lives a block over," I said. "Leona Wiley. Mrs. Sullivan might be there."

Nick raised an eyebrow. "Are you a friend of the family?"

"Leona has an account with us, too," I said.

Nick went back to asking questions. I told him everything I knew about the Sullivans, why I was at their house, what I remembered about the man who'd run into me in the living room, which wasn't much.

"He's the one who shot Mr. Sullivan, wasn't he?" I said. I was really creeped out, knowing I'd been that close to him.

"He could have been a witness," Nick said. "We won't know anything until we find him and ask him some questions."

"Didn't any of the neighbors see him leave?" I asked.

"If they did, they're not talking," Nick said.

I understood that. Devon was the kind of neighborhood where minding your own business and keeping your mouth shut could prolong your life considerably.

"Your jacket was marked into evidence," Nick said. "You'll get it back eventually."

"Keep it," I said. "Or give it to charity. I don't care."

Nick looked over the form he'd filled out, then leveled his gaze at me. "Anything else you want to tell me?" he asked.

I felt his brain-penetrating sensors boring into me. He was scanning my thoughts, searching for all the bad things I'd done in my life.

My stomach did its I'm-guilty heave.

Nick sat back and propped his foot up on the open bottom desk drawer. His good-cop pose, I guess.

"Well?" he asked.

I could feel my confession gurgling around in my stomach. I was going to tell him. I was going to admit to every bad deed I'd ever committed. I'm no good at keeping secrets. I'd have made a horrible spy.

I gulped, trying to keep my stomach where it belonged.

"Like what?" I asked, and managed to sound innocent.

"Anything you feel you should tell me," he said.

Yes, I'd done a few things, but nothing really bad. So I'd cheated on a test—it was algebra. Cheating is expected on an algebra test. And so what if I still had Lizzie Blake's CD? Who listened to N'Sync now, anyway? The lipstick theft was the worst thing I'd ever done.

No, trashing Nick's payment was the worst thing I'd ever done.

Nick leaned a little closer and mellowed his voice. "Anything you'd like to get off your conscience?"

He knew. He knew I'd thrown out his payments.

My confession pushed up from my stomach. I felt it in my chest, in my throat. It tickled the back of my mouth and danced on the end of my tongue.

I clamped my lips together and shook my head.

"Sure?" Nick asked, leaning a little closer.

I nodded quickly, refusing to open my mouth.

He looked at me a few seconds longer, then rose from his chair and said, "I'll be right back."

He left the room.

I collapsed in the chair, drained and exhausted. I wasn't meant for a life of crime. In fact, neither side of the law suited me because I sure didn't want to be in this police station any longer, giving a statement that would help the cops.

So why was I staying?

I glanced around. No sign of Nick. Nobody paid me any attention.

I hadn't been told I couldn't leave. I wasn't under arrest. As far as I knew, I was still a citizen, free to come and go as I pleased.

And right now, it pleased me to leave.

I got my purse and left.

CHAPTER THREE

I found my car parked beside the police station outside a gated lot crowded with black and white patrol cars. The doors were unlocked, my keys over the visor. I jumped in and sped away.

It's really cool to be an adult, to make your own decisions, your own choices. You can eat cookie dough for dinner or sleep on the mattress when you're too tired to put fresh sheets on.

But there were also times when being all grown up wasn't any fun at all. This was one of those times. I headed for my parents' house.

Bonita was one of the cities that adjoined Santa Flores. It spread across the base of the foothills where orange groves flourished decades ago before they were ripped out and replaced with tracts of houses. My parents lived in one of those houses in an older section that had held up well over the years.

I couldn't remember living any place else. That was the best part about going to my mom and dad's house. It was always there. They were always there. The furniture had been in the same place for years, the same family pictures hung in the hallway. Every Christmas the same decorations were on the tree. Every Easter Mom baked a cake shaped like a bunny. My dad was the only person who'd ever changed the oil in my car. He even washed it for me sometimes. He slipped me a twenty every now and then.

My parents had been married for over thirty years. They were the Mount Rushmore of parents, both carved from the same block of stone, permanently affixed side by side, forever. I found that comforting, and tonight, I needed comfort. I pulled into the driveway, parked and let myself inside with my key.

The house was a one-story with four bedrooms, a big kitchen, a den, living room, and a dining room. The lot it sat on was a little larger than most, big enough for the pool that nobody used much since my brother and I moved out.

"Mom? Dad?" I called.

My mom came down the hall from the bedrooms. A huge surge of emotion shot through me.

Mom saw me and flung out both arms.

"That father of yours! You won't believe what he's done now!"

"Well, jeez, Mom—"

"I can hardly believe it myself!" she declared. "That man!"

Mom was in her mid-fifties, tall, with brown hair and blue eyes, like me. Everyone said she looked younger, but to me, she always looked like Mom.

She stomped past me into the den. "He's really done it this time!"

I followed like a little puppy hoping for a treat. "Mom, something happened—"

"I can't live like this! Not anymore!"

"But, Mom—"

"That's it!" She drew in a big determined breath. "I'm leaving your father."

"Mom!"

"And you're helping me," she said. "Find me a moving truck."

* * *

Honestly, I didn't know how this day could get any worse, unless a meteor fell out of the sky and crushed me. At this point, that didn't seem so bad.

After Mom's announcement, I left the house under the pretense of finding a truck for her to move with. Mom acted a little weird some times, but I didn't know what this leaving-dad thing was all about. I couldn't imagine what my dad had done to drive her out of the house.

Since Dad wasn't home, I wondered if he knew what he'd done.

Mom had waved to me from the front door, told me to drive carefully, just as if nothing were different. The most frightening part of this whole deal was that one day I was going to be like that, too. I was going to get old, get weird.

I craned my neck out the window of my car and looked skyward. Where was a meteor when you needed one?

My apartment was just a couple blocks off State Street in a big complex that attracted all sorts of people—singles, young married couples with kids, old married folks with grandkids. Hardly a day went by without a moving truck blocking a chunk of the parking stalls.

I swung into my assigned spot, killed the engine and fell back in my seat. I was exhausted and hungry. I had a little headache going. The outfit I'd put on this morning—now sans jacket—that I thought had looked so awesome was wrinkled and limp. I probably smelled bad.

I dragged myself out of my car mentally preparing a plan of action once I got inside my apartment: close blinds, turn off phone, find chocolate. Maybe I'd call in sick tomorrow and sleep all day. Yeah, that sounded good.

I was just getting to the warm shower/cool sheets part of my plan when a car door opened on the other side of the parking lot and a man got out. He just stood there, watching me.

I may as well have been hit by a meteor, because that's how it felt.

It was Nick Travis. He'd come after me.

It's funny what runs through your mind in stressful situations. Seeing Nick standing outside his car, I swore not to be taken alive.

We could have a big shoot-out right there in the parking lot, except I didn't have a gun. I could make a break for the Mexican border, if I'd paid better attention in Spanish class. I could zip into L.A. and become a street person, if I didn't have such an aversion to public toilets. But I couldn't just stand there waiting to be captured.

I hitched my purse higher on my shoulder and marched over to his car.

"Go away," I said. "Go protect and serve somewhere else."

"I don't protect and serve," Nick said. "That's LAPD's motto."

"Oh. Well, what do you do?"

"Anything I want."

Nick Travis was such a dog. A mangy, flea-infested dog who deserved to be run over by a garbage truck loaded with chicken gizzards.

He leaned his elbow on his open car door and let one of his infamous grins creep over his face. It crept over me too.

He was a dog, all right, but a gorgeous one.

In matters of the heart, lighting was important. The glow of the security lamps in the parking lot softened the edges of his face making him even more handsome, if that were possible.

My lighting wish was that he couldn't see me all that well because I knew I must look pretty bad.

"We need to talk," he said

"No, we don't."

"Yes, we do," Nick said. "So what'll it be? Your place or mine?"

His place was the police station. I absolutely could not go there again.

I huffed, making sure he knew this did not suit me.

"Look," I said. "I don't have time for this. I'm hungry, tired, and I need a shower."

"I can fix one of your problems." He reached inside his car and pulled out a white paper bag. "Or fix all of them."

My knees weakened a little, but I forced myself to stay strong.

"Have you got any chocolate in there?" I asked.

"It's Chinese," he said.

"You're not going to arrest me?" I asked.

"Not tonight."

Good enough.

"You can come inside," I said. "But only because I'm hungry."

I led the way up the stairs to my apartment on the second floor, fumbled with my keys and went inside. Nick closed the door behind us.

The entry way opened to the right down the hallway that led to two bedrooms. One I slept in, the other I threw stuff into. Straight ahead was my living room, and to the left was my kitchen.

I switched on some lights and dropped my purse on the tiny kitchen table I'd wedged into one corner. Nick made himself at home opening cabinets, studying the microwave and checking out the refrigerator.

"Go take your shower," he said.

I opened the flaps on one of the little white Chinese take-out boxes. One solitary egg roll was inside. I raised an eyebrow.

Nick grinned. "Thought I'd save you from a few fat grams."

"Good of you to take the hit for me," I said. "Just don't sacrifice yourself completely while I'm in the shower."

"Then you'd better shower fast," Nick said, as he shrugged out of his sport coat and hung it on the back of a kitchen chair along with his shoulder holster.

A pleasant little meow came from under the table and my gray tabby came out, stretching and yawning. I've got the world's best cat. Sleeps a lot, eats little, likes to cuddle, and never gives unsolicited advice. What more could you ask for from a roommate?

"Come here, Seven Eleven." I picked her up and stroked her thick fur.

"You named your cat Seven Eleven?" Nick asked. "What, you found her at the convenience store?"

"And the critics said the Miss Marple story hour at the Police Academy was a waste of taxpayer money," I said, and gave him my aren't-you-clever smirk.

I got my aren't-you-clever-smirk right back.

"Hit the shower," Nick said. "And make it fast. I'm hungry."

The hot shower felt good, but it was a little strange being naked in the same apartment with Nick Travis. It occurred to me that if I stood under the water too long he might think I'd hit my head on something and was drowning, and rush into the bathroom—all in the line of duty.

That little scenario played out in my mind, and for a few seconds I considered lingering a while longer. Then I came to my senses and shut off the water, pulled on sweats and a Dodgers T-shirt, and headed for the Chinese.

Nick sat in the living room sipping a bottle of Corona from my fridge and watching television over a basket of my underwear sitting on the coffee table.

I've got a thing for underwear. The wilder the better. Prints, plaids, neon, whatever. Knowing you're walking around with zebra stripes on your butt can give you a whole different perspective on life, sometimes.

I wondered if Nick was getting a different perspective on something as he sat on my sofa looking at my front-clasp, leopard print bra dangling over the side of the basket.

I stashed the basket in the corner and sat down on the end of the sofa. Nick had brought in another beer, plates, napkins, and put it all on the coffee table with the take-out boxes. He'd already loaded his plate and had turned on the Lakers game.

"Is anything else on?" I asked, digging into the fried rice.

"You don't like basketball?" he asked.

"No," I said, tipping up a Corona. "That's one of the things I'm changing when I take over the world."

I hadn't really meant to say that out loud. People tended to look at me funny when I did.

Nick looked at me funny. "You're taking over the world?"

What could I say but, "Yes."

He digested this for a moment. "What else are you doing differently when you take over, aside from getting rid of basketball?"

Nobody had ever pursued this topic with me before, but I was ready.

"For starters, I'm taking that one really high note out of the Star Spangled Banner," I said. "You know, the la-and of the *free*. That one."

He nodded. "Makes sense. What else?"

"I'm considering banning the playing of all Barry Manilow songs," I told him, "but my mother might fight me on that one."

"A lot of mothers might."

"One thing I'm definitely doing is moving first base a foot closer to home plate," I said. "There'd be a heck of a lot more runs scored that way."

"I like baseball," Nick said.

He must have been a huge fan because his gaze lingered quite a while on the front of my Dodgers T-shirt.

When the Chinese food was gone and the beer bottles empty, we took the remains into the kitchen and dumped them into the trash. That's the kind of housework I like.

Nick leaned against the counter and gave me a stern look.

"I need you to come down tomorrow and look at mug shots," he said.

I could have protested but the beer had me feeling a little mellow. And besides, I wanted the guy who'd killed Mr. Sullivan to get caught, though I didn't think I'd be much help with the investigation.

"I don't know if I'd recognize the guy," I said. "It happened really fast, and I only got a glimpse of the side of his face."

"I want you to look at the mug shots anyway," Nick insisted. "Something might jog your memory."

I didn't like the idea that my nanosecond look at the side of some guy's face was all there was to go on.

"Don't you have any idea who shot Mr. Sullivan?" I asked.

"We haven't determined motive yet," Nick said. "We need his wife to take a look around the house, see if anything is missing."

"Have you found her yet?" I asked.

He nodded. "We caught up with her at her sister's house when they got back from shopping."

I tried to imagine what it had been like for Mrs. Sullivan to hear the news that her husband was dead—murdered. The thought made my stomach roll. It made me angry.

Nick must have noticed something from my expression.

"You stay out of this," he told me. "I don't want you poking your nose into the investigation."

"I can put my nose where ever I want," I said.

"No, you can't," Nick said. "People think that because they discovered the body or pointed out a suspect, they're involved. They want to solve the crime. They can't. You can't. This is a police investigation. Don't get in my way."

"Well, don't get in my way," I told him.

"I'll get in your way if I need to," he said.

Okay, Nick won that round—but only because he had a badge. And I was starting to feel a little loopy from the beer. And he had great eyes.

He pulled on his shoulder holster and sport coat, and headed for my front door. He paused, then withdrew a business card from his pocket.

"Call me if you remember anything," he said. "Day or night."

I took the card and saw that he'd written what must have been his personal cell phone number on it.

I opened the door. "Thanks for dinner."

"What time are you coming to the station tomorrow?" he asked.

"My lunch hour," I said.

Nick nodded and left my apartment. I closed the door and peeked out the peephole.

"Lock the door, Dana."

His voice came from the hallway.

I slid the security chain into place and peered out again. Nick was gone.

Seven Eleven rubbed against my leg. I scooped her up and went into the bathroom. I brushed my teeth while she stared at the sink, then I got into my pajamas.

In the bedroom I curled up with my pillows in the dark. Seven Eleven curled up at my feet. She usually slept at the foot of my bed, and it was nice to feel her warm little body next to me during the night.

Hers was the only warm body I'd had next to mine in a while.

That made me think of Nick.

I flopped onto my back and stared at the ceiling. I wished he hadn't come over. It's so much easier to dislike someone when you don't know them well. I wished I'd never learned he could be a nice guy.

I sighed and rolled over again. No way could I change that now. Even after I took over the world.

CHAPTER FOUR

I dragged myself out of bed the next morning and peeked through the mini blinds. Clouds darkened the sky. Rain seemed likely. Not a good way to start a day I'd rather not participate in.

Poor Mr. Sullivan lurked in my thoughts. The visage of death had been on a distant horizon for me. I didn't like the zoom lens I'd seen it through yesterday, and that I'd relived it in my dreams last night.

I'd tossed and turned, waking over and over from the same nightmare: walking into Mr. Sullivan's living room; being knocked down by the man running from the house; finding the body.

Nor could I shake the thought that if I'd arrived at the Sullivan house a minute earlier—sixty lousy seconds—it might have made a difference. If I'd turned my head sooner—only two seconds sooner—I could have seen that guy clearly and been able to give the police an accurate description, or maybe recognize him somewhere.

Of course, if I'd arrived sooner, if one single incident had been different, I might have been shot along with Mr. Sullivan. That's the thing about life—you just never knew. Good-different, bad-different, which way might it have gone?

Maybe just different enough that Mr. Sullivan would still be alive.

In the parking lot below my window, I saw the retired couple who lived below me getting into their car, probably going out for breakfast. That brought my folks to mind. I'd have to find out from Mom what was behind her wanting to leave my dad after three decades of marriage. I'd have to talk to Dad, too, and see if he had any idea what was going on. Maybe I wouldn't have to find Mom a moving van, after all.

Nick Travis bounced around in my head, though I didn't want him to. He kept popping in there, probably because of his tie to Mr. Sullivan's

25

death.

Probably.

Seven Eleven trotted along beside me as I stumbled to the kitchen. She rubbed against the cabinet door where I kept her food, and meowed her little head off.

You have to be a truly committed pet owner to face canned cat food first thing in the morning. I popped the lid and dumped it into her dish, and she happily lapped it up. When I dropped the smelly can into the trash I spotted the discarded Chinese take-out containers from last night.

It was way too early for any more deep thinking—another matter I intended to address when I took over the world—but as I sat at my kitchen table with toast and orange juice, Nick flashed in my head, followed by Mr. Sullivan, and then—ugh—Manny. How was I going to explain to him that I didn't have any money to post to the Sullivan account today—or the television he'd told me to repossess?

I forced all those thoughts away and got ready for work.

I'd rented this two-bedroom apartment with the intention of getting a roommate but before I could find anyone, the second bedroom had filled up with all kinds of things: exercise bike, skis, my desk and computer. I could have found a place for that stuff, but I couldn't do without the closet. I'd filled the walk-in in my bedroom ages ago—with clothes, of course—and was now working on the one in the second bedroom. So unless I could find a roommate content to live life with a couple of wall hooks, I was on my own.

I showered and dressed in a black and white skirt, white top, and black jacket, a suitably business-like outfit that wouldn't give our office manager Inez Marshall a heart attack—they note stuff like that in our personnel files—but then I spotted a pair of slightly slutty peek-toe stilettos. I couldn't resist—not that I tried very hard. I slipped them on and left.

As I pulled into the Mid-America parking lot it occurred to me that the shoes I'd purchased a few days ago—only marginally more slutty than the stilettos I was wearing—were still riding around in my trunk and might look even better with this outfit. I grabbed them, and went into the office.

Inez Marshall already sat at her desk, demonstrating strict adherence to her own personal policy of always arriving thirty minutes early for work. She took her responsibilities seriously.

No one else, however, took her seriously—or maybe it was just me.

If Inez had ever been married, it was decades ago. She had no children. Mid-America was her life. She'd worked there for over forty years and droned on endlessly about the old-school methods of doing business back in the day.

"You're early," Inez said, glancing at the wall clock. "We received a memo from Corporate regarding overtime. I'm covering that in my meeting today."

"And good morning to you, too, Inez," I said, as I walked past her desk.

Inez lowered her half glasses and gave my stilettos the evil eye.

"Dana," she said, "I just addressed Corporate's dress policy last week. Didn't you read my memo?"

Seven people in our office and Inez sent a memo. Good grief.

Like Inez should talk about corporate dress. Three times a year—Easter, Labor Day, and Christmas—she bought clothes. Always the same four pieces: pants with an elastic waistband, an A-lined skirt, a vest whether it was in style or not, and a jacket, all the same color. She added two blouses, a scarf and a brooch, then mixed and matched until the next holiday rolled around.

Evidently, Inez didn't own a full-length mirror or she'd be as sick of looking at the same clothes as the rest of us were. It was only late October and we'd already seen enough of Labor Day's brown-orange-yellow ensembles.

Come on, Christmas.

Inez had sent a suggestion to Corporate that the company should go with a uniform. I'd sent in a suggestion that the Employee Suggestion Program should be discontinued as it incited violence in the work place. We never heard back on either suggestion.

Corporate dress police. That's something else I'm going to change when I take over the world.

Officially, Mid-America employees reported to work at eight-thirty. We opened to the public at nine. That, according to Corporate, gave us a half hour of uninterrupted time to catch up on work, get organized, and formulate a plan for the day.

Yeah, right.

I stowed my handbag and pried the top off the shoe box only to look up and see that Inez had followed me to my desk.

"Dana," she said, taking off her glasses and letting them dangle from the chain around her neck, "as you know, I was at our district meeting yesterday and there are a number of items I need to address with you."

"If you say one more word, Inez, I'm putting this down for overtime," I told her.

She pressed her lips together and glanced again at the wall clock.

"I'll get back with you, Dana," she said, and trotted to her desk.

I spent the next few minutes trying on my new black shoes, stretching out my legs, admiring how they looked. Carmen, the branch cashier, came in—I have no idea how she always got to work on time with a child to deal with every morning—and in the middle of our discussion of heel heights, Jade Crosby arrived.

Jade was one of Mid-America's financial representatives who worked directly under Inez; it was her job to process loan applications. I didn't like Jade. I strongly suspected she'd made up her own first name probably around the time of her divorce, but that was several years before I met her, so I couldn't be sure.

What I did know for sure was that she was suspended in some sort of time warp and didn't realize she was in her thirties, had given birth to two children, and needed to buy clothes that actually fit her, rather than the sizes she'd worn in her pre-children days.

Jade wore her blonde hair long and straight. It occupied most of her time. It must have taken most of her energy, too, the way she constantly flipped her head around, swinging her hair from one shoulder to the other.

I sat behind Jade. It was like living on the set of a shampoo commercial.

She whipped her hair back and sauntered to my desk. Today she had on a knit dress that stretched tight across her butt and dipped way low in the front. Her thighs made a little swishing sound when she walked; if Spankx were under there, they weren't working.

"New shoes?" she asked.

Clever, with me scrunched down in my chair and my foot in the air, and Carmen and me talking heels.

"I got them last weekend," I said, turning my ankle right, then left.

Jade swiveled her head, swinging her hair to the other shoulder.

"I got this dress last night," she said, and ran her hands down her hips. "Size four."

Her butt hadn't seen the number four in the last decade.

"Four?" I rocked forward in my chair. "In what, Jade, dog sizes?"

She gave me another hair flip and went back to her desk.

Our front door swung open and Manny Franco hustled inside carrying a brief case and a travel mug, and looking stressed out.

"Manny," Inez said, leaping out of her desk chair in front of him. "I want to go over what I'm covering in today's office meeting."

"It's office meeting day again? Holy crap." Manny cut around her. "Whatever it is, I'll hear it in the meeting."

"But I want you to know ahead of time. After all, we are supervision," Inez said, following him to his desk.

Inez and Manny were both second in command on the office's who's-the-boss ladder of succession, with Inez in charge of lending—and also doubling as office manager—and Manny running collections. Their supervisor was Mr. Burrows, the branch manager, who had the only private office in the place and whom we almost never saw.

"I'm covering OT. Overtime," Inez went on. "That applies to your employee."

"I'm right here, Inez," I said, from my desk twelve feet away. "It's okay to use my name."

Inez ignored me, ensconced in supervisor mode big-time, and said, "Corporate is cracking down on OT. It's a controllable expense. We have to watch it."

"Dana gets the job done," Manny said. "Anybody's got a problem with her time sheet, they can talk to me."

I beamed a big smile at Inez. She gave me prune-face and went back to her desk.

At precisely 8:30, Inez rose from her chair.

"Attention, please, attention," she announced. "There will be an office meeting commencing immediately. Please gather around my desk at this time."

Inez used to use a plastic megaphone to announce her meetings until it *mysteriously* disappeared. It reappeared a day later in the closet of my second bedroom.

Carmen, Jade, and I dragged chairs to Inez's desk. Lucas Finley, the branch's other financial rep, wandered out of the breakroom, grabbed a chair and joined us. He was barely in his twenties, slender, short, had dark hair and wore glasses. Apparently he didn't own a jacket because he always wore a white shirt and one of three ties.

Lucas lusted after Jade. Something about her Betty Boop figure and Marsha Brady hair drove men crazy. Personally, I didn't get it. Jade took delight in leading Lucas on, and Lucas never realized he was being led on. I didn't get that either.

"We've just received a new memo from Corporate," Inez announced.

She turned toward Manny still seated at his desk, working.

"Manny, the meeting has begun," she called, in a voice that reminded me of my third-grade teacher.

"I can hear you," Manny said, not bothering to take his eyes off his computer screen.

"Are you sure?" Inez quizzed.

"I'm hanging on every word," he said.

Inez pursed her lips and said, "I'll cover everything with you later."

She turned to the rest of us and said, "Effective immediately, each branch will designate one employee as its safety coordinator."

Safety coordinator? This could only mean that an employee somewhere had sued Mid-America, and in typical corporate fashion, everyone up the chain of command had grossly over-reacted, causing the rest of us a lot of extra work.

"The safety coordinator will conduct safety meetings with the staff," Inez said, "and will ensure all corporate safety guidelines are met, and will report accidents or injuries to the corporate office."

Those people at Corporate. They just don't have enough to do.

Inez pulled a three-inch bound report and four packages of shrink wrapped forms from a large envelope, and thrust them at me.

"Dana will be our safety coordinator," Inez declared.

"What?"

"Look these over, Dana, and we'll have your first safety meeting tomorrow morning," Inez said.

"I don't want to be the safety coordinator," I said.

Inez looked as if she couldn't imagine why anyone wouldn't want to be the safety coordinator.

"I've already reported to Corporate," she said.

So, my fate was sealed. Shrink-wrapped and sealed, actually. I took the safety coordinator materials and glared at Carmen, Jade, and Lucas.

"I'm telling you right now," I said. "If any of you hurt yourself and cause me to have to fill out a form, I'm slashing your tires."

Inez droned on for a while longer and finally we were released from office-meeting purgatory.

"Did you get the Sullivan payment last night?" Manny asked from his desk.

"No," I said.

"You pick up the TV?"

"No."

"I'm sensing a story here." He looked over at me. "Better be a good one."

I left my desk and dropped into the chair beside his, and explained what had happened to Mr. Sullivan last night.

"Rough," Manny said, with a mournful shake of his head. "You okay?"

"I guess," I said.

"Excuse me." Inez appeared at Manny's desk. "I heard what you said, Dana. I think I should be in on this."

I saw my first safety report on the horizon.

"It's handled," Manny told her.

"First of all," Inez said, "did the customer have credit life insurance?"

I couldn't believe she'd actually said that.

"The man died, Inez," I said. "Did you miss that part?"

Inez turned to Manny. "We should advise Corporate. Dana is a witness. The legal department might need to get involved."

Manny waved her away. "Run with it, Inez."

Inez drew herself up. "I'll inform Mr. Burrows."

She approached his office door as if she was about to be interrogated by the Libyan secret police.

Most of us felt that way about going into Mr. Burrow's office.

"I have to go to the police station today to look at mug shots," I said.

"Do it with your lunch hour," Manny said.

Inez whirled away from Mr. Burrow's door.

"Actually, Manny," she said, "that would be considered Mid-American business and, as such, Dana can't do it on her lunch hour. It will put her over forty hours for the week. Overtime, Manny. Weren't you listening in my meeting?"

"No," Manny said.

Inez turned to me. "Dana, you heard what was covered in my meeting."

"I wasn't listening either," I said.

Manny turned to me, ignoring Inez.

"Go do it now," he said. "Take as long as you need."

I grabbed my things and left the office.

CHAPTER FIVE

Dark clouds gathered above the city as I pulled out of the parking lot, but rain had not yet fallen. The weather did nothing to brighten my mood. I didn't think I could face Nick Travis yet, so instead of heading for the police department I drove to Devon.

I cruised past the Sullivan house and saw yellow crime scene tape everywhere. A couple bouquets of flowers lay at the gate. Even in the Murder Capital of America, some people still cared. That was nice to know.

I drove a block over and pulled up in front of Leona Wiley's house. She and Gladys Sullivan were closer than most sisters. In fact, the whole family was close. I knew this because almost everyone in the family had taken out a loan with Mid-America at one time or another, which meant I'd collected payments from almost every person in the family.

Leona's place looked a little better than the Sullivan home. Her husband had passed on but her sons looked after her. Several cars sat in the driveway so I squeezed in at the curb. I got out and knocked on the front door.

Mrs. Wiley answered wearing a black dress, a hat with a half veil, and a somber expression. She recognized me right away.

"I wanted to tell Mrs. Sullivan how sorry I was about Mr. Sullivan," I said.

I had no intention of mentioning that I'd been at the scene of the murder. Since I didn't know any of the Sullivans' neighbors, it was doubtful that I'd been recognized leaving with the police last night. I couldn't face telling that story, then answering the questions the family surely would have.

Mrs. Wiley pulled a crumpled tissue from under the belt of her dress and dabbed at her eyes.

""Come on in, honey," she said.

Mrs. Wiley took great pride in her house. The furniture might have been old but was in excellent condition because it was covered in plastic. Clear runners crisscrossed the white carpet. The lamp shades were encased in cellophane.

"Is Mrs. Sullivan here?" I asked, stepping into the room.

"Gladys is lying down," she said. "Doctor sent over something to make her sleep."

Through an archway several people were gathered around the dining room table filled with covered dishes. I recognized some of them, Mid-America customers, members of the Sullivan-Wiley clan come to mourn and pay their respects. I waved. They waved back.

"Come sit down, honey," Mrs. Wiley said.

We settled onto her sofa, the plastic crackling under us. She patted my arm and drew in a ragged breath.

"You're so sweet to come by," she said.

I wished I could think of something comforting to say, something appropriate. But what do you say to a family when their world has been shattered? What words were good enough?

"I just can't imagine how something like this could happen," was all I managed.

Mrs. Wiley shook her head. "Me either. Arthur, he was a good man. He made his mistakes—we all did. He never got over losing his son the way he did, him going to prison and dying there."

"Leonard's father?" I asked.

She nodded. "Arthur blamed himself. That's why he was so hard on Leonard. He didn't want his only grandson to make those same mistakes."

"I'm sure Leonard appreciated Mr. Sullivan's concern," I said, because, really, I didn't know what else to say.

Mrs. Wiley touched her crumpled tissue to her eye again.

"I don't know what Gladys is going to do with Arthur gone," she said, shaking her head. "I just don't know."

"Please tell her I came by, would you?" I asked.

I couldn't shake the feeling of guilt and responsibility. It nearly choked me. All this misery, all these sad people and disrupted lives. All because I didn't arrive at the Sullivan house one minute earlier, and I hadn't turned my head to the right two seconds sooner.

"If there's anything I can do, anything at all, let me know," I said, and I'd never meant anything more in my entire life.

We rose from the sofa and I waved good-bye to the folks in the dining room. On the front porch, Mrs. Wiley thanked me again for stopping by.

"Really, if there's anything you need," I said, "just let me know."

"Thank you, honey," she said, "but I don't—well, wait a minute. Maybe there's something you can do."

Thank God. Something to do. Some way to make up for all my short-comings last night.

"Could you find Leonard?" Mrs. Wiley asked. "Nobody's seen him in a couple of days."

This surprised me because last I knew, Leonard lived with the Sullivans off and on. He changed jobs a lot, returning home through periods of unemployment. Plus, Mr. Sullivan expected him to come to the house yesterday and help out with the Mid-America payment so he could keep the television.

"I'm sure Leonard hasn't heard about what happened to his grandpa," Mrs. Wiley said. "He's got a new job somewhere, and an apartment. Got himself a new silver Lexus, too. If he'd heard what happened, he'd be here. I know he would."

"I'm sure he would," I agreed, though I thought it odd that Leonard hadn't heard the news.

"It would make Gladys feel so much better to see the boy," Mrs. Wiley said. "I know you've got ways of finding people, you know, through your job. Can you find Leonard? Tell him to come home?"

"Of course," I said. "Do you know where Leonard's working now, or where he's living?"

She shook her head. "No, I don't. But find him, okay?"

"Sure, Mrs. Wiley. I'll find him," I said.

She squeezed my hand and went back into the house. I drove away.

Part of my job as asset manager at Mid-America was to find customers who'd moved, leaving no forwarding info. As it turned out, I had a natural ability to find people—call it a gift, a superpower, whatever—but I was really good at it.

I kept this a secret—as all super heroes do—and used it as I saw fit, regardless of Mid-America's expectations.

Mostly they were folks who were hiding because they couldn't afford to pay their bills. I understood that. So once I located my customer, I'd talk to them and see what the problem was, and if their situation was legit—unemployment, medical bills, emergency expenses—I kept the info to myself with a promise from the customer to settle up with Mid-America when they could.

Unfortunately, not every customer who'd skipped out on their payments had a real, understandable reason for doing so. With them, I had no sympathy. Families were struggling to get by; I couldn't get behind somebody who didn't pay their bills just because they didn't want to.

Relieved, now, that I had something to do that would help Mrs. Sullivan, the knot of guilt in my stomach over my own shortcomings the night of the murder eased a bit. Then I remembered that I had to go see Nick, and that knot morphed into something different. I didn't know what, exactly; I decided not to contemplate that situation right now.

All I wanted to do was get to the police station, look at mug shots, spot the killer, and let that be that. End of my involvement with Nick— except to trash his payment when it came in, of course.

I sighed heavily in my silent car. Even that didn't seem like as much fun as it used to.

* * *

At the police station, Nick greeted me with a smile. Not his women-melting smile, just a pleasant, glad-to-see-you smile. This, of course, threw me off immediately.

""How are you doing?" he asked.

He seemed genuinely concerned, something else I hadn't expected.

I told him I was fine, even though I wasn't, and he took me to a little office off the squad room where a computer was set up on a table.

"Take your time," he said, as I sat down. "There's no rush."

"Any idea who the killer is?" I asked.

"We're working on leads," he answered, obviously his standard detective answer.

I'd heard that cops only liked to talk about a case to other cops, and I could understand that—up to a point. Given the circumstances, I didn't see why I couldn't know about developments in the case.

"Look," I said. "You must have learned something by now. I've come all the way down here to help out, when I should be at work—time I'm not getting paid for, by the way."

Okay, that was an out-and-out lie. So what? I wanted to know what was going on.

Still, Nick wasn't moved.

"Do I have to know some secret code word? Some mysterious hand shake?" I asked.

He stewed for a few minutes, then said, "We canvassed the neighborhood again this morning. Nobody saw anything. We're running prints, waiting for autopsy results, searching the area for the murder weapon. So far, nothing."

Okay, that was disappointing, and it made me feel a little silly for insisting on knowing.

Nick gestured to the computer. "I'll be outside if you need anything."

I watched him go to his desk and sit down. He looked comfortable, like he belonged there, wanted to be there. I guess you have to like what you're doing if you're a homicide detective in the Murder Capital of America.

I touched the keyboard—and nearly bolted from the room.

Before me was one scary mass of humanity. True, people weren't at their best after being arrested. No hair combing was permitted prior to the snap of the camera, apparently.

But still, bad hair or not, some really frightening faces stared back at me. They made me want to rush out and buy a dozen dead-bolt locks for my front door, or get an in-home job and never venture out in public again.

I paged through the pics and after a while I got used to them. I compared every face to the mental snapshot of the man who'd run into me last night. I hadn't seen much of him. He'd had on a jacket with the hood pulled up, allowing only a glimpse at the side of his face, the tip of his nose, his cheek bone and chin. Not much to go on.

Still, I flipped through all the photos. Nothing. The guy wasn't there, or if he was I hadn't seen enough of his face to recognize him.

I stood and stretched. Nick came to the doorway. His gaze dipped to my legs. A quick dip, but I saw it.

"Find something?" he asked.

I shook my head. "Sorry."

He seemed to take it in stride. I guess dead-ends came with the job.

We stood there for a minute looking at each other.

"Thanks for coming down," Nick said. He didn't move.

"Sure." I didn't move either.

Another awkward moment passed, then we both realized we were having a junior-high moment. Nick moved aside and I walked out of the room. He escorted me to the lobby, thanked me again, and I left.

Since Manny had given me free time out of the office, I saw no reason not to abuse his generosity. I headed for my parents' house.

This whole thing about Mom wanting to leave my dad seemed crazy to me. They'd been married for over thirty years. What could my dad possibly have done—that he hadn't already done at least once in all their years together?

I let myself into the house and found Mom at the kitchen counter. She gave me a hug, holding out her floured hands.

"What are you making?" I asked, pointing to the mixing bowl full of dough.

"Cookies. Another bake sale at church." She paused, then gave me her mom-look. "What's wrong? Something's wrong. You're upset. What is it?"

How does she do that? How does she always know?

Despite my initial reaction last night to run home for comfort, I'd come to my senses enough today to know I shouldn't tell Mom about the murder I'd walked in on. I didn't want her to get started on my job again, or on me moving back home and allowing her and Dad to pay my college tuition. They'd offered before, but I refused to put that financial burden on them.

"It's you and Dad," I said, which was a partial truth.

"Oh." She turned back to her dough. "Did you get a truck?"

"What's going on with you and Dad?" I asked.

"That father of yours, honestly," she grumbled. "I just can't live like this anymore. Do you know what he wants now? Did he tell you?"

She didn't wait for me to answer.

"Satellite TV." Mom flung out both hands. "Satellite TV with all those sports packages, and old movie channels. And for what? So he can watch television—more television."

My dad was a couch potato. His idea of exercise was taking another lap around the salad bar. But he'd always been this way, so I wasn't sure how an upgraded TV package had escalated the situation to this extreme.

Mom turned back to the dough. "We used to do things, your father and me. Now all he does is sit and watch television. It's like he's rooted to that recliner. If he gets more channels to watch, we'll never go anywhere."

I couldn't disagree with Mom on this one.

"Have you talked to Dad about it?" I asked.

"Why should I have to talk to him? Can't he see I'm bored? Can't he see that he's wasting his life—and mine?" she asked.

Having Mount Rushmore parents was a wonderful thing. They were stable. They could be counted on. The drawback was that nothing carved from stone could talk.

"I need that truck," Mom said. "I'm not staying in this house."

"Where are you going to go?" I asked.

"I'll find an apartment somewhere," she said. Her face brightened. "Oh, I know what I'll do."

I saw this one coming like a star ship jumping to light speed.

"Wait, Mom—"

"I can stay with you."

"No, Mom—"

"You have that second bedroom," she said.

"It doesn't have a bed in it!" I forced myself to calm down. "Look, Mom, you can't jump into this without knowing where you're going."

She sighed heavily. "Maybe I'll stay with Aunt Jean."

"Maybe you could just talk to Dad."

She dismissed my advice with a wave of her hand. "I need that truck."

I couldn't fight her. Mom was Mom.

"Okay, I'll handle it," I said.

I drove away from the house wondering how long I could put off finding her a truck. I needed to talk to Dad and see if I could work out something between them. This wasn't easy for me. My people skills were lacking, at times. Believe me, I'm the last person a hostage wants negotiating for their release. Still, I was going to have to figure out something.

But first, I had to find Leonard Sullivan.

It seemed odd to me that no one in the family—and it was a big family—had been able to contact Leonard and tell him about his grandfather's death, even if he did have a new job and his own place, as Mrs. Wiley had said. And of all the times for Leonard to be in accessible, why now?

Still, I was glad to do Mrs. Wiley the favor.

A little chill swept up my spine as I pulled into the office parking lot. The last person I'd done a favor for was Mr. Sullivan.

And he'd ended up dead.

CHAPTER SIX

"I need you to do a property inspection," Manny said, when I sat down at my desk the next morning, feeling pretty good wearing a new pair of gray pants and a sort-of new sweater.

It seemed Manny had expended his maximum compassion for my finding a dead body while on the job when he'd let me take a long lunch to look at mug shots yesterday. Now it was business as usual.

"It's the Griffin account out in Webster," Manny went on. "We're looking at a possible foreclosure."

I've done property inspections before, but I never liked them. No way did I want to be involved with someone losing their home, no matter how small a part I played—especially now, with Mr. Sullivan's murder stuck in my head, along with Nick Travis, of course.

"What's up with the Parker auto?" Manny asked, shuffling papers around on his desk.

"Jarrod Parker, that idiot," I mumbled.

Jarrod Parker was definitely not one of the Mid-America customers whom I'd felt deserved my own personal twist on my job requirements. He had a solid position with an engineering firm. He made an excellent salary. He had the capacity to pay—he just refused to do so. With so many families struggling, yet still managing to pay their bills, I didn't have a lot of patience for somebody like Jarrod.

In the afterglow of ecstasy, apparently, Jarrod had co-signed a loan for his girlfriend and put up the title to his car for collateral. She skipped, which left him responsible for the payments. Jarrod didn't see it that way. Since his girlfriend had gotten the loan proceeds, he didn't think he should have to pay.

I tried to reason with him. I'd explained that, regardless of who got

39

what, he was legally responsible for the debt because he'd signed the loan documents. Still, he'd refused to pay. But he hadn't stopped there. He'd made it personal. He'd crossed the line. Granted, it was my own personally drawn line, but he'd crossed it just the same. In fact, he'd blown right by it.

I get some angry customers—although that wasn't mentioned in my initial job interview with Mid-America—but Jarrod had escalated from anger to name calling, then cursing and threats, all directed at me. I'd ordered the repossession of his car—our collateral—in the hope it would convince him to make the payments. I didn't want his car, I just wanted him to pay off his account and go away.

The repo agency, however, hadn't been able to find his car. I'd been looking for it, too. I kept the pertinent info in my car and often cruised past his house hoping to spot it. No luck, so far.

"I'll call and see if there's anything new to report," I told Manny.

He rose from his chair, picked up his briefcase, then dropped a folder on my desk.

"Get on this. I've got the district meeting in Riverside," he said, and left the office

I looked at the label on the file folder and saw it was the possible foreclosure on Griffin account. No way did I want to deal with that now.

Even though most of our work was done on the computer, we had a physical file for every customer that contained their legal contract, supporting documents, and any correspondence. I pulled Leonard Sullivan's folder from the file cabinet and took it back to my desk.

Leona Wiley had told me that Leonard had a new job and residence. It had been my experience that searching the past was a good way to find someone in the present. When people lost their job, they often went back to a place they'd already worked—don't ask me why; you'll never catch me piercing ears at the mall again—so I phoned the previous job listed on Leonard's loan application. No luck. He hadn't returned to work there and the guy who'd answered the phone had no idea where he was. I called his previous landlord and struck out again. Leonard had moved out several months ago and had left no forwarding address.

I located Leonard's personal reference sheet in the file—info customers voluntarily give us when they're pleased with our service and are okay with us contacting friends and family to solicit their business— and saw that he'd listed a number of relatives. A few of them I knew because they'd had loans with Mid-America. Some I didn't. I phoned them all and learned nothing new. No one had seen Leonard. No one knew where to find him.

I was getting nowhere. Maybe I wasn't concentrating. Maybe I wasn't trying hard enough. Maybe I was missing something obvious.

I sat at my desk contemplating these possibilities, wondering if—after I found Leonard, discovered Mr. Sullivan's murderer, and got a handle on my feelings about Nick—I should consider searching for another job. A major life change might be in order. A move, maybe? Another town, another state?

This probably wasn't the best time to make the leap, with the economy being what it was. Still, it was nice to think about—except that, as always, I came up short on one important issue—what career did I want? Sooner or later I was going to finish my B.A. so I'd have to come up with something.

Nothing that required extended stretches behind a desk; I can't sit still that long. I didn't have any technical skills. My stint piercing ears at the mall was as close as I ever wanted to come to the medical profession.

What about something totally out-there, like the arts? I mentally took stock of my natural artistic abilities. I'd been the head fairy in my ballet recital, but that was when I was five years old, and the only dancing I'd done since then was a vague recollection of a pole and tequila shots at a bachelorette party. I could sing pretty well, as long as the shower thundered around me. Unless I could find a gallery willing to sponsor a showing of Crayola Washable Marker, I wasn't likely to make it as a painter.

Inez walked up to my desk, shattering my perfectly good daydream.

"I discussed your involvement in the Sullivan murder with legal," she said. "I told them you'll write up your statement and email it to them right away."

That settled it. I needed a job with a gun.

"I'm not doing that," I said. "Not until I discuss it with my personal attorney."

I didn't actually have a personal attorney, but oh well.

Inez pressed her lips together. "You'll advise me when you've done that?"

"As soon as I talk to my lawyer," I said, "you'll be the first to know."

She trotted away and I slumped farther into my desk, annoyed with Inez, annoyed with Nick for not giving me any info on the murder, but mostly annoyed with myself for not finding Leonard yet.

I grabbed my purse and the two file folders on my desk, and left.

* * *

I drove to Webster, a rural, agricultural area about twenty minutes east of Santa Flores, and found the house Manny wanted me to inspect.

It was a custom job designed to resemble an old Victorian but was really only two years old, situated on a half-acre, wooded lot. It seemed deserted, even though a red Mustang with the customized plate BN THERE sat in the driveway. According to the file, Sean and Belinda Griffin had two daughters, probably in school.

I really didn't want to be here, doing this, even though all I had to do was walk through the house and make sure it was in good condition. Mid-America needed that info before deciding whether or not to foreclose. If the place had been trashed and would require mega bucks to repair, then Corporate needed to know that; it might effect their decision on what to do with the Griffin account.

I couldn't bring myself to get out of the car just yet. The weight I'd been carrying around with me since I'd found Mr. Sullivan's body seemed to be holding me in my seat.

A sweeter man than Mr. Sullivan, I'd never known. Completely harmless. Old. No physical threat to anyone. So why would anyone have killed him? And not just killed him, but walked into his own house and shot him at point blank range. Twice.

The image of the bedroom I'd found him in flashed in my head. Neat, orderly. Nothing out of place. No struggle. Cold, calculated. This was no crime of passion. Somebody wanted Mr. Sullivan dead. What could he have done to arouse such violence in someone?

It was hard to imagine that Mr. Sullivan had an enemy or a dispute with a neighbor or family member that would cause this. A gang initiation, maybe? It was common—terrible, but common.

And what about the guy I'd seen running from the house? It was easy to think he'd been the shooter, but maybe he wasn't. An accomplice? Or, like me, someone who had wandered into the house, discovered Mr. Sullivan's body, then taken off, fearful he'd be considered a suspect.

The front door had been ajar when I'd arrived. Did that mean the guy who'd actually murdered Mr. Sullivan had run out earlier and failed to close the door? That scenario gave credence to the theory that the guy who'd run into me had wandered inside later, after the shooting. Plus, the guy didn't have a gun—at least, not one that I'd seen.

I gazed across the wooded lot into the trees and decided I shouldn't put too much emphasis on the tall white guy who'd knocked me down. If I kept too narrow a view of the crime, I might miss the big picture.

I pushed the whole thing out of my head, forcing myself to get back to work. I opened the Griffin file and took a minute to look it over.

Sean and Belinda Griffin had taken out a second mortgage loan from Mid-America about a year ago for home improvements. Sean worked as a factory foreman in Ontario, about forty-five minutes from here, and

Belinda was a housewife.

Their trouble started seven months ago when they began making their payments late, then skipping payments altogether. Currently, they were four payments behind. Manny—he handled all the mortgage accounts in our office—had attempted to contact the Griffins a zillion times to try and work something out, but hadn't gotten a response.

I flipped through the file and saw the new credit report Manny had obtained a few days ago. The Griffins' owed everybody. Twenty credit cards, all with huge credit limits, all maxed out. No wonder they couldn't pay their mortgage.

I got out of my car, snapped a picture of the house with my cell phone, and walked up to the front door expecting to be on my way again after a knock or two. To my surprise, a woman answered.

"Belinda Griffin?" I asked.

"Yes," she replied.

She was in her late twenties, blond, attractive, well dressed for a woman alone in the house during the day. Her hair and nails were done. She had on a skirt and sweater, and pumps.

I introduced myself and handed her my business card. Belinda shrugged and stepped back from the door. I went inside.

From the high balances on her many credit cards I'd expected that Belinda spent her days at the mall and her nights glued to the shopping networks. But the house was barely decorated. Average furniture, a hodge-podge of pictures and floral swags on the walls. "Uninspired," my mother would have called it.

I followed Belinda to the kitchen. She scrounged through her purse on the counter. I hoped she'd dig up the cash to bring her account current, but all she produced was a hair brush, a dozen Lottery scratchers, and a pack of cigarettes.

"What's the deal?" Belinda asked and lit up.

"The company is considering foreclosure," I said. "I just need to take a look at the house."

I'd said those words to customers before and I got a variety of responses in return. Shock, disbelief, panic, fear. Belinda just shrugged.

"Go ahead. Look all you want," she said, and blew out a puff of smoke. "There's nobody here."

I took a look out the kitchen window into the backyard. According to the file, Mid-America had loaned the Griffins' money for a patio, patio cover, built-in barbecue and landscaping. I was pleased to see they'd actually had the work done; it would improve our chances of selling the property, if it came to that.

I went upstairs noting that, like the first floor, not much effort had been put into fixing up the place. When I got back to the living room, Belinda was lighting another cigarette.

"You've got a nice place here," I said when I reached the front door. "I'd hate to see you lose it."

She drew in a big breath of smoke, then let it out slowly. "Do what you have to do."

I couldn't let it go at that.

"Would you like me to come back later and talk to your husband about this?" I asked. Sean worked on an assembly line and wasn't allowed to take phone calls. According to the file, no one from Mid-America had spoken with him.

"Sean doesn't want to discuss it," Belinda said.

I felt more concerned about the Griffins' losing their home than Belinda seemed to be.

"Don't you care about keeping your home?" I asked.

She shrugged. "It's just a house."

I wondered if her two little girls felt the same way. I wondered how she could put so much money and effort into buying the home, then let it go with so little thought.

"If your situation changes, Belinda, and you come into some money, call the office right away," I said. "There's still time to save your house."

She shrugged. I got in my car and drove away, not feeling so great. I didn't like doing property inspections, but it was more than that. Something with Belinda. I just couldn't put my finger on it.

I wound my way back to the 10 freeway and headed west toward Santa Flores. But instead of exiting on Fifth Street to go back to the office, I kept going. I'd found the name and address of Leonard Sullivan's cousin, Todd Murphy, on his personal reference sheet in his file, and decided that paying a visit in person might produce more info than a phone call.

I exited the freeway a few minutes later in Atwood. The neighborhood looked a little scary. Fences were tagged with graffiti, abandoned cars sat on vacant lots, houses were run down, their yards overgrown.

My GPS took me to the Murphy home. I parked at the curb and walked up to the front door. Windows stood open and I heard water running inside.

I knocked and a few minutes later, a tall black woman in her fifties opened the door wiping her hands on a dishtowel. She did not look happy to see me.

I introduced myself, and said, "I'm looking for Todd Murphy."

"Todd's my boy." She narrowed her eyes at me. "What do you want with him?"

"Actually, I'm trying to find Leonard Sullivan," I said. "He gave Todd as a reference."

Mrs. Murphy swelled like a Mylar balloon, and for an instant I thought her eyes might shoot out of her head.

"I've got nothing to do with that Leonard Sullivan," she declared. "My boy Todd knows better than that."

"Isn't Leonard your nephew?" I asked.

Mrs. Murphy planted her fists on her hips. "He's my nephew—technically. But I don't claim him. I don't claim any of those Sullivans. Trouble. Everyone of them is nothing but trouble. Including that Arthur. It doesn't surprise me one bit what happened to him. Not one bit."

My stomach did a little flip. "You're not surprised he was murdered?"

"Arthur caused trouble, just like his boy, just like his grandson," Mrs. Murphy said. "It wasn't a month ago that there was a big stink over Arthur and one of Gladys's friends. Embarrassing, that's what it was. A man his age carrying on with another woman—right in his own neighborhood."

I gasped. "Mr. Sullivan had a girlfriend?"

"A *married* girlfriend." Mrs. Murphy jerked her chin. "Her husband put a stop to it. Lord, that man was mad, the way I heard it. Shameful, that's what it was. Shameful and disgusting."

"Who's the woman?" I asked.

Mrs. Murphy's pursed her lips. "That Ida Mayhew. She's nothing but trouble—just like Arthur. That husband of hers has his hands full with her—always has."

I hadn't expected to hear any of this. I gave myself a mental shake to recall why I'd come here in the first place.

"I'm trying to find Leonard," I said. "Have you seen him?"

Mrs. Murphy calmed down a little. "I've heard nothing from Leonard in months, and that suits me just fine."

I pulled a business card from my purse and passed it to her.

"If you hear from him, would you ask him to call?" I said.

"If I see him," Mrs. Murphy said, and disappeared into the house.

I was stunned. Mr. Sullivan had been involved with another woman? A married woman? What other secrets did that family have?

When I reached my car, I could see that I'd attracted the attention of a group of young black guys two doors down. I drove over and buzzed open my window.

"Hey," I called. "Where's Leonard?"

They were in their late teens, dressed in baggy pants and oversized shirts. They looked at each other, then grinned and sauntered to my car.

"Looks like Leonard's got himself a white girl," one of them said.

The others laughed and it seemed I'd become their amusement for the day. Okay by me, as long as I got the info I wanted.

"So where is he?" I asked.

One of them leaned down and rested his arm on the window of my car.

"Leonard don't hang here no more," he said. "He's got himself new friends. He came around here driving a big-ass Lexus and flashing some serious cash."

"When?" I asked.

"Couple of days ago," the guy said.

"I heard he's got a new job," I said.

The three guys laughed, and the one hanging on my car window said, "Oh, yeah. Leonard's got him a job, all right."

"If you see him, tell him Dana's looking for him," I said, and passed him a business card.

He took it and backed away from the car.

"Thanks," I called and drove off.

I hadn't found Leonard, but I'd found a motive for murder.

CHAPTER SEVEN

When I arrived at the office Manny hadn't returned from Riverside yet, so I saw no reason to attend to my official duties. Despite picking up an unsavory bit of info about Mr. Sullivan and one of his neighbors, I hadn't accomplished much in my search for Leonard. Everyone I'd spoken with had said that he hung with a different crowd, had a new job, a new home, an expensive car, and was flashing some serious cash, which meant I wasn't likely to find him through my contacts with his family.

Of course, I couldn't ignore the motive I'd discovered for Mr. Sullivan's murder—his married girlfriend who came complete with a jealous husband.

Since Mrs. Murphy had provided me only with the woman's name, I had some digging to do. I phoned the title company Mid-America did business with and asked for a list of all properties owned by one Ida Mayhew. The clerk gave me one address, owned jointly with Ida's husband, Gerald Mayhew.

I waited until I saw Inez pick up her phone to make a call.

"I'm going out," I said, as I breezed past her desk.

I drove to the Mayhew home, which was located down the block from the Wiley house. Like most of the houses in the neighborhood, the place looked a little run down. I parked in the driveway alongside an SUV, grabbed one of the file folders off my passenger seat, and knocked on the front door. A gray-haired, African-American man—I put his age at mid-sixties—opened the door. He was dressed in work clothes; despite his age, he looked fit, muscular and strong.

He gave me a look of deep suspicion, which I'd seen many times since taking this job with Mid-America.

47

I introduced myself and told him where I worked, then flipped open the file folder.

"I'd like to speak with Will Saunders," I said, giving him the name I'd made up on the drive over.

"Nobody here by that name," he said, and tried to close the door.

"There's supposed to be," I said, sounding confused. "This account was transferred to our office and it gives this address as Will Saunders' home. Is he a friend or relative of yours?"

"Never heard of him."

"Well, he's giving out your address," I said, with a suggestive eyebrow bob.

"Somebody's giving out my address?" he demanded, edging closer to see inside the folder.

"If this is an error, I can correct it," I said, closing the folder. "If I could see your I.D., I can assure my supervisor you're not the man we're looking for."

He thought for a few seconds while I tried to look innocent, then pulled his wallet from his hip pocket and flipped it open displaying his driver's license. He was Gerald Mayhew, all right. And next to his license in a separate plastic sleeve was an employee identification card from Fowler Security Service.

"You work for Fowler?" I asked, sounding chatty. "I hear it's a good company. Have you worked here long?"

"About ten years," Mr. Mayhew said, tucking his wallet into his pocket.

"Do you know Dan Hollister?" I asked, pulling the name out of thin air. "He works for Fowler at the mall."

"Don't know him."

I nodded thoughtfully. "You must have been worried the other night, with the shooting just around the corner."

Mr. Mayhew bristled. "I was working that night."

I backed up a step. "Well, sorry to bother you. I'll get this account corrected right away."

"Good," he said, and started into his house.

"Do all the security guards at Fowler carry a gun?" I asked.

"Of course," he said, and looked a little surprised by my question.

I nodded and went back to my car. When I pulled away, Gerald Mayhew was still standing on his porch watching me.

The thought of going back to the office was even more unappealing than usual, so I circled the block and pulled into Leona Wiley's driveway. I wanted to let her know about my efforts to locate Leonard, such as they were. I also hoped she could give me the low-down on

Arthur Sullivan and Ida Mayhew.

Mrs. Wiley welcomed me into the living room, offered me a cup of tea, which I declined, and we sat together on her couch. The house was empty and quiet, just the ticking of a clock somewhere and the crackle of plastic beneath us.

I updated her on my attempt to find her wayward nephew, and she thanked me three different times. She was so nice about it, I felt even worse for having failed so miserably.

"I understand there was a misunderstanding between Mr. Sullivan and one of his neighbors," I said, trying to phrase my comment as delicately as possible. "Gerald Mayhew and his wife."

Mrs. Wiley's lips turned down distastefully. "Wasn't nothing to that. Not really. Not on Arthur's part, anyway. Arthur used to drive us ladies to bingo every week."

"That doesn't sound like a big deal," I said.

"Ida, she's always making something out of nothing," Mrs. Wiley said. "She got that husband of hers all stirred up, trying to make him jealous. But Arthur, he didn't want trouble so he quit driving us to bingo. Leonard took over about a month or so ago."

"Do you think Gerald Mayhew carried a grudge?" I asked.

"He's a hot-head." Mrs. Wiley gasped and clasped her hands together. "You don't think he could have shot Arthur, do you?"

I was saved from answering when Gladys Sullivan shuffled into the room dressed in a floral housecoat and fuzzy slippers.

Leona hurried to her, caught her arm, and helped her sit down in the chair beside the couch.

"Look who's here," Leona said, gesturing to me, attempting to make me sound like something interesting. "I'll go fix you some tea, Gladys. Just rest right here."

The wing-back chair seemed to swallow Mrs. Sullivan. She looked a little out of it, and I wondered if she was still taking the sedatives the doctor had sent. She seemed thin and drawn, more wrinkled than I remembered, as if she'd aged another sixty years since Mr. Sullivan's death.

Silence stretched endlessly in the room while I wracked my brain trying to think of something appropriate to say. Mrs. Sullivan didn't seem to care if anyone spoke or not, which should have been a relief, yet somehow it increased my sense of guilt and responsibility over her husband's death and my inability to locate her grandson, the one person who might actually bring her a little comfort.

I was contemplating making a break for the door when Mrs. Sullivan spoke.

"Leona said you were going to bring Leonard home," she said.

This wasn't the conversation I was hoping for.

Mrs. Sullivan squeezed her eyes shut. Tears rolled down her cheeks.

"He's just scared, that's all," she said.

She'd spoken so softly, I wasn't sure I'd heard her correctly. I slid off the couch and onto the footstool beside her chair.

"Who's scared?" I asked. "Leonard?"

Mrs. Sullivan pulled a crumpled tissue from the pocket of her housecoat and wiped her tears.

"Arthur and Leonard, they had a terrible fight," she said. "My Lord, the things they said to each other. Turned my blood cold."

"When?" I asked.

"That afternoon." Mrs. Sullivan sniffed. "Arthur said he'd go to the police himself before he'd let Leonard end up in trouble. And Leonard said---"

I leaned forward so far I almost fell off the footstool.

"What did Leonard say?" I asked.

"I don't know." Mrs. Sullivan shook her head. "I couldn't stand to hear them going at each other like that. My Lord, the words they used on each other. I left. I just left the house and came over here to Leona's, and we went to the store."

I couldn't think of anything to say.

"He's just scared," Mrs. Sullivan said. "Leonard loved his grandpa, and the last time they were together, they fought something fierce. Leonard thinks I'm mad at him, or he's ashamed of himself, or worried what the family might think if they found out about him and Arthur arguing that way."

"Did you tell anyone about the fight?" I asked.

"Oh, no. No, I didn't. I don't want anybody thinking bad of Leonard." She took my hand and squeezed it. "You find Leonard for me. Tell him it's okay. Tell him everything is okay."

"I will," I promised.

Leona came into the room with a tea tray and plate of cookies. I extracted myself from Mrs. Sullivan's death grip, said what I hoped was an appropriate farewell, and left.

So Mr. Sullivan and Leonard had a terrible argument. Threats had been made shortly before the murder.

I was okay with Gerald Mayhew being a suspect. But Leonard? The victim's own grandson? A guy I knew and liked?

Things like that just shouldn't happen.

I've really got my work cut out for me when I take over the world.

* * *

When I arrived at the office Manny had returned from Riverside and was working at his desk.

"Where have you been?" he asked, as I walked past.

I glanced at Inez. She'd ratted me out.

"I phoned Jarrod Parker at his job but he wasn't in," I said. "I thought he might be home so I drove over to see if his car was there so I could have Quality Recovery pick it up."

The lie rolled easily off my tongue. Manny shrugged and turned back to his computer.

I shuffled papers across my desk, pretending to work, and wondering if I should call Nick and give him the info I'd gleaned about Mr. Sullivan's murder. Maybe, in return, he'd tell me what he'd uncovered.

It was worth a try.

I phoned his office but he wasn't in so I left a message. At that point, there was nothing to do but get to work, which seemed kind of okay, given the day I'd had so far.

I pulled up the Griffins account and downloaded the photo I'd taken of their soon-to-be-foreclosed house, and wrote up my comments on the inspection I'd done. Because I'd lied to Manny earlier about Jarrod Parker's car, I decided to redeem myself by actually calling the repo agency and seeing if they'd had any luck finding the car.

My good intentions were shattered before I picked up the phone. Inez loomed over my desk.

"Dana, we're ready for your safety report," she said.

"My what?"

Inez pulled off her glasses. "Now, Dana, don't tell me you didn't read the safety materials the corporate office sent."

I stole a quick glance at the stack of shrink-wrapped forms Inez had presented me with that I'd put on the floor and kicked under my desk.

"Of course I read them," I told her.

"Did you find them useful?" she asked.

So far, they made a great footrest.

"Very useful," I said.

"We're ready for your report," Inez said.

I hadn't read the material—and I had no intention of doing so.

"If you'd read Corporate's memo carefully, Inez," I said, "you'd have seen that, as branch safety coordinator, I'm required to conduct a safety inspection prior to giving my safety presentation."

"Oh?" Inez peered around my desk trying to spot the safety packet.

I eased it a little farther under my desk.

"My inspection will be completed today," I told her.

"Well, of course," Inez said, squaring her shoulders. "If that's what Corporate wants."

Inez went back to her desk and I headed for Manny.

"You've got to do something," I whispered, dropping into the chair beside his desk. "Inez has got me doing some stupid safety thing for Corporate."

Manny closed his eyes for a few seconds and shook his head.

"Do it, Dana," he said. "It's from Corporate."

With no one else to complain to and no hope of a reprieve, I went back to my desk, dug out the corporate office's safety materials and flipped through them. Sure enough, there was an inspection I had to perform.

I've worked for this company way too long.

I found a clipboard in the stock room, clamped my inspection report to it, and set about making our office a safer work environment.

Manny and Carmen's work areas were free of violations, and I awarded them the safety smiley-face sticker that Corporate had included with my materials. Lucas's desk grossed me out when I found a half eaten Pop Tart in his top drawer, so I moved on. I searched my safety checklist for a hair net requirement but couldn't find one, leaving me no choice but to give Jade a passing grade.

At Inez's desk, I poked and peered around, shaking my head and making the most annoying *tsking* noise I could manage.

"You're a real hazard, Inez," I said. "Corporate will have to hear about this."

"What? But, Dana—"

"Just doing my duty." I dropped to my knees and crawled under her desk. "More than three plugs in an outlet. We can't allow that, Inez." I yanked the plugs, disconnecting her computer and calculator.

I was liking this job. If only it came with a gun.

I crawled out from under her desk and tapped my pen against the clipboard.

"You're in violation of section 2.10 of the safety inspection, Inez," I said, and pointed to her personal-sized oscillating fan. "Exposed cord. That's another write-up. Jeez, Inez, are you trying to kill us all?"

"But, Dana, how am I supposed to work without my computer and my calculator?" she asked.

"Not my problem." I peeled a big red sticker from the safety materials folder and slapped it on her desk. "But you can't work here until these safety issues are corrected and have been re-inspected."

"Very well." Inez drew herself up and lifted her chin. "If Corporate so dictates, then it must be done."

"Damn straight." I snapped my clipboard and went back to my desk.

I enjoyed an Inez-free afternoon while she scoured the stores in Santa Flores for the items necessary to bring her work area up to code. I managed to look busy enough that Manny didn't give me so much as a glance, so it seemed like a great time to take a break.

The office breakroom was adequate, with a small refrigerator, a microwave, sink, and vending machine. I got a soda, sat down at the table, and helped myself to the newspaper someone—probably Lucas— had left there.

I found a small article about Mr. Sullivan's death on page four, with a quote from Detective Nick Travis stating the police were following up several leads but had no suspects. The article also reported that Mr. Sullivan's funeral was scheduled for next week.

The whole thing seemed sort of low key. That bothered me. From living, breathing human being to a statistic. Sad.

Definitely worth changing when I took over the world.

CHAPTER EIGHT

I called it a day, glad to be out of the office, anxious to go home, but not free to do so. My work still wasn't done.

I drove to my parents' house and found the garage door open and Dad at his workbench. He was still a nice looking man, even with a little gray at his temples and a few lines on his face; his couch-potato lifestyle showed around his middle.

Gerald Mayhew flashed in my mind. Could he actually get so jealous that he'd do bodily harm to Mr. Sullivan? At his age, wouldn't he be over all that territorial stuff by now?

I sat in my car for a few minutes watching Dad puttering at his workbench and thought about him and Mom, and all the years they'd been married. If love was strong enough to keep two people together for decades, was it strong enough to commit murder for?

"What's wrong with your mother?" Dad asked as I walked up.

"Don't you know?" I asked.

"How would I know?" he said. "She's not talking to me. Gave me a grilled cheese sandwich for dinner and took off for her sister's house."

Mom prided herself on putting together creative—though sometimes quirky—meals. If she was dishing out sandwiches, she might be more serious about moving out than I'd hoped and this wasn't a problem that would likely blow over. I didn't like to get involved in my parents' personal life, but I knew I had to jump in.

"She's upset about the TV sports package you want go get," I said.

Dad seemed confused for a few seconds, then shrugged. "If she doesn't want the sports package, then we wouldn't get it. End of story."

"I'm afraid it's not that easy," I said. "Mom wants to go out more. She's bored sitting at home all the time."

"She gets out," Dad said. "She's at her sister's right now, isn't she?"

"She wants to go with you," I said. "She told me you two used to do lots of things together."

"We do things," Dad insisted. "Just the other day we … we, ah …. Huh. I could have sworn we did something."

"She thinks life is passing her by," I said.

Dad heaved a long sigh. "Talk to her, will you? She'll listen to you."

"I tried," I said. "You're going to have to do something. Take her out. Go places with her."

Dad looked totally lost. "Go places? Where?"

Now I was almost as annoyed with Dad as my mom was.

"Where did you used to take her?" I asked. "You know, back when you were dating."

He grinned. "I used to take her out to the orange groves after dark. We'd back in between the rows and—"

"Stop!" I put up my hand. What was it with parents? Just because you became a mature adult they thought you wanted to hear stuff like that?

After my stomach stopped rolling, I went on.

"Okay, Dad, you've got the idea here, I said. "Just go do things."

I gave him a peck on the cheek and left feeling a little better about life. My parents weren't on the road to reconciliation yet, but at least they were pointed in the right direction—which meant I wouldn't have to find a truck for Mom to move in. I headed home.

At my apartment complex I swung into my designated spot and got out of my car. The security lights cast shadows across the parking lot. I looked around. No sign of Nick tonight—which was a good thing. Wasn't it?

I climbed the stairs to my apartment and found Nick on the floor, leaned back against my door, tie pulled down, collar open. He was reading the newspaper and eating a chicken leg.

My heart jumped into my throat, even though I didn't want it to.

"What are you doing here?" I asked.

He looked up. "You called me."

"That was hours ago," I said, recalling that I'd phoned him from the office earlier. "Good thing I wasn't on fire."

Nick picked up the grease-stained bag beside him. "I brought dinner."

"Isn't there some place you're supposed to be?" I asked.

"Like where?" he asked.

I wasn't sure I could handle another clueless man tonight.

"Home," I said. "Your home."

"No," he said.

"Isn't someone expecting you?" I asked.

Nick picked up another bag. "I brought ice cream."

My resistance started to shake. Nick saw it.

He rattled the bag and said, "Chocolate, chocolate chip."

I crumbled. I'm so shallow sometimes.

"You can come in," I said. "But only because you've caught me at a weak moment."

Again. I seemed to be having a lot of those lately.

I let us into my apartment. Nick headed for the fridge while I went to the bedroom. I changed into jeans and a sweater, then joined him in the kitchen.

Seven Eleven sat at Nick's feet looking up at him with big green eyes, and meowing her little head off. It gave me pause. Was that how I looked when I gazed at Nick?

I hoped not.

We filled our plates with chicken and fixings and ate in front of the TV, then hit the ice cream.

"So, what's up? Why did you call me?" Nick asked, as he scraped the last chocolate chip from his bowl.

I'd phoned Nick this afternoon hoping to trade info about Mr. Sullivan's murder. I had more information than I knew what to do with—a possible affair, a jealous husband who was a security guard and owned a gun, a missing person who'd been overheard arguing with the deceased.

But now, looking across the couch at Nick, I wasn't sure how much— if any—of this information I should share with him. For one thing, since he was the homicide detective assigned to the case he probably knew all of this and if I spilled my guts I'd end up looking like an idiot. And if he didn't already know, my telling him might get some innocent person in trouble, or send the investigation down a dead end, wasting Nick's time and possibly allowing the real murderer to escape. And, if Nick knew I was involved in the case, he might refuse to give me any info at all.

I'm definitely making decisions less complicated when I take over the world.

"I wanted to see how the Sullivan case is going," I said, thinking it best not to give anything away.

Nick must have also thought it best not to give anything away because he said, "We're continuing the investigation."

"You sound a little vague," I said.

"You sound like my lieutenant."

Nick gathered the plates and went into the kitchen. I picked up our trash and followed.

"Did you find the murder weapon?" I asked, trying to sound chatty as we straightened up with kitchen.

"No."

"Do you have any suspects?"

"No."

"Any new leads?"

"No."

"Have you found a motive?"

"No."

These less than informative answers didn't suit me. I was getting nowhere. Time to try another tact.

I mentally debated the three time-honored feminine methods of gaining a man's cooperation—whining, crying, or offering sex.

I couldn't bring myself to whine to Nick, and I didn't think I could work up any tears unless I poked myself in the eye. That left sex, and somehow I sensed that once we went there, the very last thing on my mind would be Mr. Sullivan's murder investigation.

I huffed impatiently.

"Okay, look," I said. "You're just being annoying. What's the big deal about me knowing what's going on with the investigation?"

Nick stared down at me, cold and unmoved.

"Well?" I demanded, trying to appear as cold and unmoved as he.

After a few more seconds of glaring, Nick relented.

"We got fingerprints from the Sullivan house," he said. "Family, and a building contractor. Only one of them had a criminal record. Leonard Sullivan."

"Leonard?"

I couldn't hide my shock. I had no idea he'd been in trouble with the law. To me, he was a nice, likable guy who had trouble keeping a job and paying his bills on time.

"What sort of criminal record?" I asked.

"Drug possession, assault, some juvenile stuff," Nick said. "Nothing stuck. No convictions."

"Have you spoken with Leonard?" I asked. If he had, he could tell me where to find him.

"We haven't located him," Nick said.

"What about the other prints?" I asked.

"A building contractor named Kirk Redmond," Nick said. "I spoke with him this morning. He was at the Sullivan house about a week ago giving an estimate for some painting."

Another dead end.

I thought about Gerald Mayhew.

"What about the neighbors?" I asked,

Nick shook his head, then said. "Your prints were there."

I gasped. Of course, my fingerprints would have been found at the crime scene, but it was a little uncomfortable knowing I was part of the official investigation.

Nick touched my chin and turned my face up to his.

"Anything else you want to know, Nancy Drew?" he asked.

My universe narrowed and every thought flew out of my head. This was nice. Me standing close to Nick. Him smelling good. His hand touching my chin. The kind of nice I could get used to.

But I didn't dare.

I pulled back.

"What are you doing here?" I asked. "Here in Santa Flores, I mean. Where have you been since high school?"

"New York," he said.

"Why did you come back?"

Nick gave me a lopsided grin. "I missed the place."

He was blowing off my questions, and I didn't like it.

"Tell me the truth," I told him. "I want to know."

Nick leaned back against the kitchen counter and studied my face, as if deciding whether he should share this information with me.

"I worked undercover in New York," he finally said. "I saw ugly things, Dana. A lot of ugly things. My folks still live here. I wanted to come home."

I didn't think it could be that simple.

"That's it?" I asked.

"That's it," he said.

"Who's waiting for you at home?" I asked.

I knew this was a stretch, really none of my business. But I asked anyway.

"Nobody," Nick said. "Nobody is waiting."

"No wife? Fiancé?"

He shook his head.

I decided to push a little further, since he was in a cooperative mood.

"What about a girlfriend?" I asked.

He didn't hesitate.

"Nope. No girlfriend," he said.

A little wave of relief washed over me.

"What about you?" he asked and gestured toward the back of my apartment. "Husband? Fiancé?"

"No," I said, feeling another wave of *something* spread through me.

"Boyfriend?" he asked.

I shook my head.

"So does this mean I can come by and bring you ice cream again?" he asked.

My knees weakened and my heart started to beat a little faster.

"As long as it's chocolate," I said.

A little grin crept over Nick's face. I hadn't seen this one before. I couldn't interpret it.

He headed for the entry way. I followed and opened the door.

"Thanks for dinner," I said.

The words came out sounding softer than I'd meant for them to.

"You're welcome."

His words sounded softer, too—or maybe that was my imagination.

He left. I closed the door and slid the security chain into place, then squinted into the peephole. Nick stood in my hallway grinning smugly and waving.

That dog. He knew I'd look at him.

I went to bed.

CHAPTER NINE

My headlights cut through the pre-dawn darkness as I turned onto the long, gravel road that led to Quality Recovery and my opportunity to elicit some justice from the small world in which I lived.

After the last few days, I figured I was due.

If I hadn't known where to find this place, I'd have driven right past. Quality Recovery wasn't the kind of company that advertised.

Abandoned cars littered the overgrown fields on each side of the narrow road, along with some dilapidated sheds tagged with graffiti. Quality came into view, lit up like a football stadium. Banks of security lights beamed down on a couple of tin roofed buildings that were surrounded by a twelve-foot chain link fence topped with razor wire; two big German shepherds prowled the lot.

Inside sat rows of neatly parked cars—Mercedes, Beemers, Caddies, Chevys, Fords, most every make—all "recovered" by Quality Recovery.

A tow truck idled outside the gate, gray exhaust rolling out the back. I parked, grabbed my things, and climbed into the passenger side of the truck; even though I was officially on company business, I had on jeans and a sweatshirt.

"Morning," I said, settling into the seat.

"Hey."

The voice that spoke from the semi-darkness on the other side of the truck belonged to Slade, one of Quality Recovery's agents, known less politically correct as a repo guy.

Slade was ex-Air Force Special Ops. Big—well over six feet—and muscular. His blond hair was cut short. I guessed his age at around thirty, but it was hard to tell. He had an earring. Tattoos, too, I guessed, but I'd never seen any. Not that I hadn't wished I could look.

I'd known Slade since I started the job at Mid-America. Strictly professional, of course. This was the first time he'd taken me out with him to pick up a vehicle. It was the first time I'd ever asked to go along, the first time I'd ever wanted to go along.

Some things in life you've just got to be there for.

Quality Recovery was a part-time gig for Slade. Nobody seemed sure what he did when he wasn't picking up vehicles, but drug cartels in Mexico and terrorism in the Middle East came to mind.

"I brought coffee and doughnuts," I said.

"Cool."

I passed him a cream-filled—keeping the chocolate for myself—and one of the coffees I'd picked up at Starbucks.

"Got the docs?" he asked, finishing off the doughnut in two bites.

I waved the file folder, then read off the street address. He punched it into his GPS and we drove away.

"What's the story?" Slade asked.

Around a mouth full of doughnut, I explained about Jarrod Parker's girlfriend who'd skipped, and that Parker had refused to pay.

"Dumb-ass," Slade mumbled. "What are we looking for?"

"A Mustang convertible," I said. "Yellow."

"You spotted it?" he asked.

"At his house a few hours ago," I said.

I'd seen Jarrod Parker at a club last night. After Nick left, I'd tried to sleep but couldn't, so I called my BFF Jillian Brown—we've know each other since high school—and we decided to go out.

It wasn't unusual for me to see one of my Mid-America customers somewhere. The company had thousands of clients and Santa Flores wasn't that big.

"Jarrod was drinking last night, really pounding them down. He's probably out cold," I said.

Slade glanced at me. "You performing services above and beyond?"

"No way."

"Just checking," Slade said. "Don't want to walk into some domestic thing."

A few minutes later we turned onto Emerald Avenue. Slade killed the headlights and pulled over to the curb. The street was only a couple of blocks long, lined with tract homes, a nice middle-class neighborhood that had been around for over twenty years.

"Got it," Slade said.

Squinting into the darkness, I spotted the yellow Mustang parked at the curb in front of Jarrod Parker's house. Anger flew through me. People were out of work, upside down on their houses, struggling with high gas prices, accepting whatever jobs they could get just to put food on their tables. Families were making hard decisions about what they could do without. Christmas was coming and some parents weren't going to be able to put a lot of gifts under their trees.

And there was Jarrod Parker, a guy with a steady job, great income, not a lot of debt, and few responsibilities who refused to pay his bill because he didn't want to. No way was I letting him get away with it, which was why I wanted to be here when Quality picked up his car.

When I'd spotted him last night he'd been drinking heavily and hanging onto every chick who passed by, completely recovered, it seemed, from the heart break of the girlfriend who'd dumped him, skipped out, and left him with Mid-America's loan payment. While everyone else had crowded the bar and pushed their way to the dance floor, I'd run into the parking lot and found Jarrod's Mustang. I'd considered calling Quality right then but had decided against it; too many people around, if things went sideways.

So this morning I hauled myself out of bed and drove to Jarrod's place. Sure enough, there it sat right in front of his house. He'd been too tired or too drunk to put it in the garage.

I glanced at Slade. He studied the neighborhood, the houses, the other cars parked nearby.

These repo guys were some bad dudes. Most of them weren't in it for the money, just the rush. Things could get crazy during a recovery. A nosy neighbor might call the police. The vehicle owner might take offense to seeing his car being towed away and come out swinging—or shooting.

Slade had a cell phone clipped to his belt. That's how I'd contacted him this morning after I'd driven past Jarrod's house. I was pretty sure he had a gun on him, too.

He turned to me. "Ready?"

Not as ready as Slade, but I'd probably never be that ready.

"Let's do it," I said.

A few houses had porch lamps burning and fewer still had lights glowing in the windows, as we crept down the street. The darkness was just beginning to dissolve into gray.

Slade swung the tow truck in front of the Mustang. The idea was to get in, hook the car, and get out quickly. Speed counted. Slade exploded out the door.

My heart banged in my chest. The adrenaline rush caused me to shake. I twisted in my seat keeping watch for a neighbor or a police car.

Slade was a madman. He zinged around the front of the Mustang hooking it up to the tow truck like the Tasmanian devil on a sugar high.

I gulped a few times, thinking we'd make it. We'd pop this car, get away clean, and leave Jarrod to wonder what the heck was going on when he got up late and tried to get to work on time—without his car.

My little piece of justice loomed within my grasp when the front door bust open and Jarrod came outside.

Slade saw him first. By the time I scrambled out of the truck they were in a stand-off on the sidewalk. I rounded the truck and he turned on me.

"You bitch!" Jarrod started toward me.

Slade drove his fist into Jarrod's chest, knocking him back a step. Jarrod wasn't much bigger than me; dressed in jeans he must have pulled on before he ran out of the house, he looked sickly white under the security lighting.

He stumbled, then took another look a Slade, then at me. I could see he was working on one whale of a hangover. He mumbled a couple of sentences. Slade took a step closer, and that seemed to take the fight out of him.

"Ah, come on, man, you can't take my car," Jarrod said, whining like a little girl.

"You should have made your payments," I said.

Jarrod mumbled something else I couldn't understand, which I suppose was for the best.

Slade kept an eye on us and went back to hooking up the Mustang.

"Okay, okay, I'll pay you," Jarrod said, raking his hands through his hair. "How much is it?"

"Call it seventy-four hundred and some change," I said.

He let loose with another mouthful of curses, then said, "I'll get my checkbook."

"Forget it," I said. "I need cash."

"Cash?" His gaze drilled me. "You think I've got that kind of money lying around?"

I shrugged. No way was I taking a personal check from him.

"What's it going to be?" Slade asked.

I looked at Jarrod. He dragged his hands down his face and started cursing again.

"We're out of here," I said.

I climbed into the tow truck with Slade and we pulled away dragging Jarrod Parker's shiny yellow Mustang convertible behind us.

By the time Slade and I got back to Quality's recovery yard and I wrote up my vehicle inspection report on the Mustang, I had just enough time to go home, change clothes, and get to work. For a moment I fantasized about walking into the office wearing my jeans and sweatshirt, which would likely bring Inez to a full-blown stroke. While it seemed appealing, I didn't want to be greedy; repoing Jarrod's Mustang was enough for me today.

I drove home, changed into khaki pants and a red sweater, fed Seven Eleven, and left. I considered phoning Nick. I wasn't sure but something might have happened between us in my kitchen last night, and I toyed with the idea of pursuing it. Then the image of Katie Jo Miller came into my thoughts and the notion of calling Nick flew right out. Besides, he had a murder to solve—in the Murder Capital of America— and by comparison, my world was a small, which suited me just fine at the moment.

When I walked into the office Inez was already seated at her desk, just like one of those snarling dogs waiting at the gates of Hell. Everyone else was getting coffee from the breakroom and settling in for the day.

"I'm ready for re-inspection," Inez announced.

At first I didn't know what she was talking about, then she gestured to the multi-plug outlet under her desk.

"I bought a new fan, too," Inez said. "No more frayed wires. The office is now safe."

Unless Corporate authorized gun carrying.

I ripped the red sticker off her desk and said, "Your name will have to appear in my report to Corporate because of the violations."

"Yes," she said. "I understand."

She would.

I helped myself to coffee from the breakroom, then stopped by Manny's desk.

"Quality picked up Jarrod Parker's car this morning," I said, thinking it better not to mention my role in the repossession.

He grunted—which was about as pleased as Manny ever got over anything—and I went to my desk. I entered the info on the repossession in the computer, then decided to spend my morning on my own personal pursuits. I'd given enough to Mid-America already today.

So far, Gerald Mayhew was the only person I knew who had an actual, verifiable motive for killing Mr. Sullivan. Even Nick hadn't uncovered a motive, according to what he'd told me last night. But Mayhew also had an alibi—or so he claimed.

I accessed the Internet and phoned the Human Resources department at Fowler Security Service. The clerk I spoke with verified that Gerald Mayhew was currently employed as a security guard assigned to the evening shift at the Stanford Medical Clinic on Dayton Avenue in Santa Flores. This type of call was routine. Mid-America, and most every other financial institution, called to verify employment as part of the credit approval process.

I hung up, a little disappointed that Mayhew's alibi had panned out because my only remaining suspect was Leonard Sullivan. Leonard, who'd had a terrible argument with Mr. Sullivan the afternoon of the murder, an argument over something that had prompted Mr. Sullivan to threaten to call the police. Leonard, who had a criminal record. Leonard, who hadn't been seen since the argument.

I didn't want it to be Leonard.

I remembered Nick had told me that another set of fingerprints was found in Mr. Sullivan's house. They belonging to a building contractor named Kirk Redmond who'd claimed he'd been at the Sullivan home to give an estimate on some painting.

This didn't sit right with me. The Sullivans didn't have money to pay their bills, and could barely afford to buy Mrs. Sullivan's medicine. Would they really have wanted their house painted?

I'd only worked at Mid-America for a short while but I had occasionally run into customers who did things that didn't make sense concerning their financial situation. But the Sullivans didn't strike me as those kinds of customers.

Of course, I didn't think Mr. Sullivan would have carried on with a married woman either.

I accessed the Internet once more and checked out Kirk Redmond's web site. His office was located in Hayward, a small town just east of Santa Flores. I dug a little more and found what I figured was his home address, also in Hayward. I emailed the info to my Hotmail account. I made a phone call to the title company and learned that, according to county records, Kirk Redmond owned no property.

So now I knew where he worked and probably lived, but what good that would do, I had no idea.

"I'm going to Quality Recovery to do Jarrod Parker's vehicle inspection," I said, which was a lie, but a believable one.

I'm pretty sure I saw Manny nod as I breezed past his desk.

I drove to Leona Wiley's house. Gladys Sullivan answered the door. She didn't look any better than the last time I saw her. We sat at the kitchen table and struggled through small talk before I came to the point of my visit.

"Did you and Mr. Sullivan plan to have your house painted?" I asked.

"We talked about it," she said, apparently not wondering why I'd come by to ask such an odd question.

"Did someone come out and give you an estimate?" I asked.

"Not that I know of," she said. Tears clouded her eyes. "But maybe

Arthur wanted to surprise me."

Oh, no. I'd made her cry. I didn't want her to cry.

"Can I get you some tea?" I asked.

I'd heard women offer tea to each other in times of stress. I didn't know what good it did—give me a beer anytime—but I was floundering here.

Thankfully, Mrs. Sullivan pulled herself together and sniffed back her tears.

"No, honey, I'm fine," she said. "You run on now. I know you've got to get back to work."

Leona Wiley appeared from the kitchen, so I didn't feel too guilty about leaving Mrs. Sullivan after I'd upset her.

In my car I thought about how I'd gotten exactly the info I'd been after. I wasn't happy about it, though.

According to Mrs. Sullivan, it was entirely possible Kirk Redmond had come to the house and given a painting estimate. Plus, he had no motive for shooting Mr. Sullivan that I knew of—or could even imagine, for that matter. Nick hadn't mentioned one, either.

With Gerald Mayhew's alibi intact and Kirk Redmond out of the picture, that left only one suspect—Leonard Sullivan.

* * *

When I walked into the office Carmen popped up from her chair behind the front counter.

"Guess who's here?" she whispered.

"Jarrod Parker?" I asked, hoping he'd come in with cash to pay off his account and redeem his Mustang.

"His car was repossessed?" she asked.

"This morning," I said. "Did he come in while I was gone?"

Carmen shook her head. Since she handled all the cash that came into the office, she'd know whether or not Jarrod had been in—and the first to know when he walked through our front door.

"When he shows his face here, I need to speak with him myself," I said. "Don't let Manny have him. He's mine."

"Okay, sure." Carmen's smile returned. "Guess who's here."

She looked a little too happy for our surprise guest to be auditors or our distract manager.

"Slade," she said, with a dreamy look on her face.

Thoughts of murder suspects and repossessed autos flew out of my head.

"He's in the breakroom," Carmen said. "With Jade."

I felt very territorial all of a sudden. I tossed my purse on my desk and headed for the breakroom.

Not that I really needed another reason to dislike Jade, but she had two children whom she ignored. They were little. The only quality time Jade spent with them was on the drive to and from the babysitter. That's just not right.

Definitely an issue I intend to address when I take over the world.

I stopped at the door of the breakroom. They were there, all right. Just the two of them.

Slade stood beside the water cooler holding one of those little paper cups. It looked ridiculous in his hand, a hand meant for gripping beer bottles with broken necks, and automatic weapons. Jade was beside him making really irritating girl noises.

I had to break this up—if for no other reason than that Jade would need a neck brace from all the hair-swinging going on.

"Jade," I said in my businesslike voice. "You have a phone call."

She glanced back at me. "Take a message, hon."

No way was I going to let that go by unchallenged.

"It's an emergency," I said. "Your babysitter."

Okay, that was a lie. But desperate measures were called for here. She had no business talking to Slade. Slade was mine. Well, not mine-mine. But more mine than hers. We'd repo'd a car together. We had history.

Jade rolled her eyes and uttered a long-suffering sigh, indicating she was *so* important, with *so* many important matters to attend to.

"See you Saturday night," she said, and left after one final hair flip.

"Hi," I said and walked into the breakroom.

"Hey."

"How's it going?" I asked.

"Cool."

Slade wasn't much for conversation. But we all have our strengths, and his was his looks. I'd settle for that.

"Brought you the inspection report on the Mustang," Slade said. "On your desk."

Even though I'd written up a report of my own on the condition of Jarrod Parker's car when it was repossessed, Quality Recovery compiled one also to cover them after the vehicle was left in their storage yard.

"He hasn't been in to pick up his car," I said, "which means he didn't have money to cover the check he tried to give me. He was going to stiff me."

"Bastard," Slade grumbled.

With that, our conversation ran out. It's hard doing it one-sided.

"I'll let you know if he redeems the car," I said.

"Cool."

We walked through the office and out the front door. Traffic on Fifth Street whizzed past.

An idea popped into my head, so I ran with it.

"Do you know anything about a contractor out in Hayward named Kirk Redmond?" I asked.

Slade just looked at me. At times I wasn't sure if he was slow-witted, or just careful about every response he uttered.

"My folks want some work done on their house," I said, feeling pressured to fill the silence.

"Don't know Redmond," Slade said. "I'll ask around."

We stood there for a minute looking at each other.

"So, you and Jade are going out?" I asked, doing my best to sound only casually interested.

He shrugged. "We're hanging out."

Everybody knew what that meant.

"Saturday night, huh? That's good," I said. "Maybe her yeast infection will clear up by then." I gave him a big smile. "Well, bye."

I went back into the office. Jade glared at me when I passed her desk.

"That wasn't my babysitter." She started talking so fast and high-pitched it sounded like she was speaking Farsi, or something.

The afternoon dragged by and finally it was time to go home. In my car I cranked up my CD player and lowered the windows. Cool night air blew my hair around.

Friday, over and done with. Another week in the books. I settled back in my seat and took stock.

On the plus side, I'd possibly saved my parents' marriage, consoled a bereaved family, and made Inez Marshall's life miserable for a while.

On the down side, I'd stumbled onto a murder, threatened foreclosure, and narrowed down several murder suspects to the one person I truly didn't want to be involved.

And I'd gotten to know Nick Travis; I wasn't sure how I felt about that.

It had been one heck of a week. I was glad it was over. On to the weekend.

I swung into my parking space at my apartment complex. No strange cars were in the lot. No Nick offering Chinese food.

I climbed the stairs to my apartment. No smell of chicken in the hallway. No Nick.

I unlocked my door and went inside, not sure why I felt disappointed.

CHAPTER TEN

Why was it so much easier to get up early on Saturday than during the week?

I contemplated this weighty issue as I pulled on sweats and put my hair in a ponytail bright and early on Saturday morning. Seven Eleven seemed less concerned about life, as I emptied a can of Kitty Stew into her dish and gave her some fresh water. I pulled on a jacket, grabbed my iPod, and left my apartment.

At the bottom of the staircase I tightened the laces on my running shoes, settled the ear buds in place, switched on Three Days Grace, and off I went.

I'm not big on exercising. I went to the gym a couple of times a week, but I didn't especially like it. I loved running.

I jogged through the maze of sidewalks that crisscrossed the complex, then took to the driveway, bobbing my head and firming my thighs.

Another thing I liked about running was the solitude, the peace of those empty-headed moments with nothing important to think about.

But for some reason, unwanted thoughts kept drifting through my brain this morning. Namely, Nick Travis.

When I got home last night and hadn't found Nick in my driveway or outside my door, I'd been disappointed. At first I told myself it was because I'd been hungry and he'd brought dinner two nights this week. But now, in the warm light of the morning sun, I had to admit my disappointment stemmed from something deeper. Something beyond chocolate, chocolate-chip ice cream.

Jogging down the driveway I considered this situation. To be honest with myself, I accepted that I'd had a terrible crush on Nick when we were in high school. He hadn't known I was alive, of course.

And as long as I was being honest, I admitted that I'd been a little jealous of Katie Jo Miller when the two of them started going out. Then she'd gotten pregnant, and I'd gotten angry—at Nick.

Of course, that was a long time ago. I'd changed. Katie Jo had probably changed. Nick might have changed.

I circled the far end of the parking lot and headed toward my apartment again. Maybe Nick really was a nice guy now. He'd been nice the last few times I'd seen him. Maybe the years had changed him.

Or maybe I was expecting Nick to be something he just couldn't be. Like when we were in high school.

I didn't want to be disappointed all over again.

I'd jogged about a mile by the time I returned to my apartment, short of breath and knees aquiver. Just as I grabbed an energy bar from the cabinet, my cell phone rang. It was my best friend, Jillian Brown.

"Want to go shopping?" she asked.

I was always up for a trip to the mall—especially if it helped rid my brain of thoughts of Nick, and Mr. Sullivan's murder.

"We need costumes," she said.

Halloween was a week away. If we wanted an awesome costume— and who didn't—we couldn't wait until the last minute.

"I'll pick you up," I said, then ran through the shower, got dressed and left.

Jillian and I had been friends since high school. She had big brown eyes, and dark hair with an auburn tint to it, and had a job at a bank in Santa Flores and an apartment not far from mine. She dashed out as I pulled up. Both of us were wearing the same sort of outfit—jeans, sweater—but since Jillian is five inches shorter than me, it came off differently.

"What are you going to be for Halloween this year?" Jillian asked as we pulled up in front of the costume shop on State Street that had been there for decades.

"I thought I'd get inspired," I announced, as we went inside.

Easy enough to do. Costumes hung on dozens of racks down the center of the store and along two of the walls. Another wall held accessories. The place smelled like lint and wood floors.

"Our costumes have to be fabulous," Jillian said. "Nothing less will do for Felderman's party."

Between Jillian and I, we knew lots of people, most of whom liked to party. So far, we'd been invited to three parties next Saturday night. Halloween was on the following Monday, so everybody would be celebrating the weekend before. Costumes required.

The best party, by far, was given by Ron Felderman. He lived in the upscale area of Maywood, just east of Santa Flores, and threw a Halloween bash to die for. Everybody was there. The party routinely spilled out of the house, onto the lawn and into the street. Things got pretty wild.

"What do you think?" Jillian asked, holding a Snow White outfit in front of her.

"Dream on," I said. "I held up a black and white striped prison uniform. "Maybe I'll wear this to work."

Jillian rolled her eyes. "And give Inez a heart attack?"

"Call it an early Christmas present," I said.

We went through another rack considering the possibilities and I decided to talk to Jillian about the situation still clinging to the back of my mind.

"Do you remember Nick Travis from high school?" I asked.

She looked at me over a set of green hospital scrubs. "Are you kidding? Who could forget Nick Travis?"

"I saw him the other day."

Her eyes rounded. "Nick Travis? You saw Nick Travis? Oh my God, what did he look like? Is he still gorgeous? Oh, he is, isn't he?"

"He's still good looking," I said. "Do you remember what happened with him and Katie Jo Miller?"

"You mean Katie Jo getting pregnant?" Jillian's mouth dropped open. "That was Nick? Nick got her pregnant?"

"You didn't know that?"

"Oh my God. You're kidding. Nick Travis got Katie Jo Miller pregnant?"

"It was all over school," I said. "I thought you knew."

"There were rumors, but I never knew for sure," Jillian said. "Katie Jo got really weird after that happened."

"She didn't want to be friends anymore," I said.

"What's Nick doing now?" she asked.

"He's a cop."

"Yeah?" Jillian seemed lost in thought for a few seconds, then said, "Whatever happened to Katie Jo?"

"I never heard anything about her after high school," I said.

"I wonder if she ever thinks about Nick," Jillian said.

I wondered if Nick ever thought about Katie Jo.

After an hour of digging through costumes, we made our selections and left. Come next Saturday night, Jillian would be the fairest damsel in the land, and I, the sassiest pirate who never sailed the Seven Seas.

We decided that we'd hit Club Vibe, a great place off Clayton Boulevard, later tonight. I dropped her off and drove to my parents' house.

While I didn't expect my efforts at marriage counseling to have solved my folks' problems completely, I did expect to at least find them together. They weren't.

So much for my career as a social worker.

Dad was in his bedroom standing in front of the mirror, swathed in powder blue polyester.

"Is that a leisure suit?" I asked.

Dad preened in front of the mirror. "Still looks pretty good, huh?"

"Well ..."

"Fits good too," he said, stretching the button toward the button hole. "Your old dad's still got it."

I was completely lost.

"What's going on?" I asked.

"Just doing what you said." Dad leaned a little closer to the mirror and smoothed back his hair. "You're right. Your mother and I need to get out more."

"You're not going to wear that suit, are you?" I asked.

He squared his shoulders. "Your mother loves me in this suit."

Who was I to argue with that?"

"Where's Mom?" I asked.

"Down at the church," he said. "Some bake sale, or something."

Good. As long as she wasn't at the U-Haul rental place.

I leaned against the door casing. "Do you remember Nick Travis? I went to high school with him."

"Nope," he said, shaking his head. "Don't remember."

"He got Katie Jo Miller pregnant," I explained.

"Who's Katie Jo Miller?"

"My best friend, Dad," I said.

That whole incident had devastated my sophomore year. How could my dad have forgotten?

"Nick Travis," I said again. "He played football."

"Oh, *that* Nick Travis. What a quarterback. Boy, that kid could throw a ball. Hit the receiver right at the goal line the last five seconds of the game that won the division championship." Dad looked at me. "He got somebody pregnant?"

"I thought maybe you remembered some of the parents talking about it," I said.

He shook his head. "Nope. Not a word."

I made myself a sandwich hoping Mom would come home. I wanted to talk to her and see how things were really going with Dad. She didn't show up so I left, content that Dad was on the right path, leisure suit and all.

* * *

Club Vibe was huge, and always packed. I slid my car keys and some cash into the pocket of my skirt, and Jillian and I got in line at the entrance. Two bouncers worked the door. One patted down the men, the other checked women's purses.

We moved inside with the flow of people. The place was packed. The deejay played Pitbull while a couple dozen people danced. The music was loud, the room dark, the crowd close. Jillian and I had discussed strategy on the drive over, noting who to look for, who to avoid. It was dollar drink night until 11:00. Anyone wanting to get drunk on a budget would have to do it quickly.

We made our way to one of the bars, bought beer, then proceeded to the most important part of the evening—seeing who was there.

Jillian and I wove through the crowd, and wouldn't you know it, the first familiar face I saw was Jarrod Parker's.

"Hey, Jarrod," I called. "I didn't know the city bus ran past this place."

Jarrod stopped, and instead of being angry he looked me up and down, and smiled. *That* kind of smile.

Jeez, what was up with this guy? The last time I'd seen him, I was repossessing his car, his only transportation, and he'd called me some very colorful, if unimaginative, names. And just now I'd thrown the whole incident in his face with a really snotty comment, which I probably shouldn't have done, but he didn't seem to notice.

"Hey, Dana," Jarrod said, easing closer. "You're looking good tonight."

One beer didn't get me drunk enough to fall for that old line—especially coming from this guy. I'd never get that drunk.

"Are you going to pick up your Mustang, or what?" I asked.

Jarrod tipped up his beer and grinned. "You've been thinking about me, haven't you?"

"Yeah," I told him. "There's something about a jackass who won't pay his bill that I can't get off of my mind."

Okay, that too was a really crappy thing to say. But it seemed to entice him, somehow.

I just don't get men sometimes.

"Want to dance?" Jarrod asked.

"Maybe in my next life," I told him, and left him with that goofy grin on his face, holding his beer.

Jillian took off after some guy she knew so I circulated, talking to people I recognized. I came to this club pretty often so I'd gotten to know a lot of people. Other faces looked familiar, but I couldn't place them.

By the time I found Jillian again, she'd gotten ahead of me on beers and was out of money. I volunteered to get more cash out of her purse— we'd locked them both in the trunk of my car—so I left my drink in her custody and headed out to the parking lot.

After the press of hot bodies inside the club, the air felt chilly. Music drifted out, melding with the buzz of cars on the street.

I hurried across the lot to the last row where I'd parked my car, popped the trunk and reached inside.

Somebody grabbed me from behind.

CHAPTER ELEVEN

A big hand clamped onto my arm, spun me around, and shoved me against my car. I tried to pull away but he squeezed tighter, quelling my adrenaline rush with raw fear.

He was a black guy so tall I had to lean my head back to look at him. He had on sunglasses, a dark overcoat, and a knit hat pulled down to his eyebrows.

Who was he? What did he want? How could this be happening—to me? My mind screamed a thousand questions in a nanosecond.

"You listen to this good, bitch, because I'm not repeating myself." He leaned closer. "What happened to old man Sullivan is none of your business. You keep your ass away from it. Got me?"

I was trembling so hard I must have nodded "yes." Good thing, because I couldn't have spoken a word if my life depended on it—which, I believed, it did.

He gave my arm a final squeeze, then whirled around and disappeared between the cars.

I didn't stand there long enough to see what happened to him. My heart pumped like crazy. My arms and legs shook. And I was freezing.

I grabbed our two purses from the trunk of my Honda, slammed the lid and ran back into the club.

My whole body trembled as I wove through the crowd to the hallway outside the restrooms and dug my cell phone from my purse. I wanted out of this place. I wanted to go somewhere safe. But I was too scared to go into the parking lot again.

I had to call somebody. But who?

My dad? Good grief, no.

The police? Yeah, I could call them but what would I say? That I'd been frightened in the parking lot? Big deal. It was Saturday night in the Murder Capital of America. No way were they rushing right over.

Nick Travis? Oh, Nick. Yes, yes, yes.

Nick was the perfect person to call. He'd be here in a heartbeat. He'd help me. He'd—

No, not Nick. No, no, no. Calling Nick would escalate our relationship to another level. It would acknowledge that we did, in fact, have a relationship.

Or that we didn't, if he failed to rush to my rescue.

Either way, I wasn't ready to turn to Nick—which left only one person.

I scrolled through the address book in my cell phone and called Slade.

It's kind of interesting what you'll bargain away in times of need. By the time the call went through I'd sworn off drinking, vowed to go to church every Sunday, and was ready to deal away my first born child.

"Hey."

Slade's voice spoke in my ear. My knees nearly gave out.

"I need your help. I'm at Club Vibe and some guy jumped me in the parking lot and—"

"On my way."

The call clicked off. I stared at my phone for a few second, then dropped it in my purse.

I didn't know where Slade was or how long it would take him to get here—or if he'd even made sense out of my hysterical ranting—but I wanted to take off as soon as he arrived.

I found Jillian at a table near the dance floor sitting with two girls whom, I recalled, worked with her. I handed over her purse.

"I'm sick," I said shouting over the music.

She squinted in the dim light and said, "You don't look so good."

"I'm going home," I said. "Can you get a ride?"

"You can ride with me," one of the other girls said.

"No," Jillian said. "You're not feeling good. I'll take you home."

No way was I going to allow Jillian to walk into that dark parking lot with me. Plus, once we got outside I might burst into tears, and I didn't want to go into the whole Sullivan murder thing with her.

"Stay. Have fun. I'll be fine," I insisted, then darted away before she could say anything, and waited by the front door for Slade.

I expected him to roll up in an Abrams tank, or a Hummer, at least. Instead he pulled up in a black Blazer, left it at the curb, nodded to the bouncers and headed toward me.

I'd never been so glad to see anyone in my life.

"You hurt?" he asked.

"Just scared," I said.

"That's cool, babe."

Slade hooked my elbow and we walked outside. He opened the passenger side door, helped me climb in, then took a look around the parking lot before getting behind the wheel.

I pointed out the back window. "My car—"

"Got it covered," he said.

I didn't know what that meant, exactly, but I let it go.

"What's the story?" Slade asked, pulling out of the parking lot.

"A few days ago I witnessed a murder, sort of," I said. "Some guy jumped me in the parking lot and told me to mind my own business."

Slade glanced at me but didn't ask anything else. He drove to my apartment keeping an eye on the road and the rearview mirror. Slade walked me inside. I expected him to leave but instead he took my key, told me to wait in the hall, and went in ahead of me.

I didn't stay in the hall. In the entry way I saw him flipping on lights, checking out each room. He came back, closed and locked the door, and slid the safety chain into place.

At this point, the incident in the parking lot seemed surreal. Looking back, I felt kind of foolish that I'd been so frightened, that I'd panicked and called Slade.

I went into the kitchen. He followed and leaned against the door casing, crossing his arms over his chest.

I knew I owed him more of an explanation, so I told him in detail about my involvement with Mr. Sullivan's death. Slade seemed to know about the murder, and I got the feeling it wasn't from the newspaper accounts.

I thought I was doing pretty well until I got to the part about tonight's incident. Tears suddenly popped up in my eyes. I tried gulping them down but more kept coming. I didn't want to cry. I didn't want to admit to myself that the jerk in the parking lot had that much control over me. I didn't want to fall apart in front of Slade.

I brushed away my tears, gulped hard, and forced myself to go on.

"It wasn't such a big deal, really," I managed to say. "I mean, the guy didn't hurt me, or … or …"

Slade came forward. He put his arms around me and pulled me against his chest.

I lost it. I cried and sobbed. Slade just stood there. He didn't move, didn't say a word.

The thing about men was that they were always trying to fix things— a holdover from some ancient hunting instinct, I suppose. If a woman had a problem, she could hardly get the words out before the guy was steam rolling her with the solution.

Slade wasn't like that. He just held me and let me cry. I hadn't pegged him for Mr. Sensitive, but he was doing a darn good job.

When I finished crying, I was exhausted. Not one single emotion or one ounce of strength remained in me. Slade guided me to my bedroom and pulled back the covers on my bed. I felt his hands on the button at the back of my skirt.

"Are you planning to take advantage of this situation?" I asked.

"Wouldn't be cool," he said.

"Darn ..."

He unfastened my skirt and let it fall, then pulled off my sweater. I sat on the edge of my bed and he yanked off my shoes.

"You'll be safe here tonight," Slade said. "I'm staying."

I lay back on the bed and said, "Are you sure you're not going to take advantage of this situation?"

He grinned and pulled the covers over me. "Go to sleep."

He switched off the light and left.

I fell asleep.

* * *

The green numerals on my alarm clock told me noon approached when I awoke the next day. I laid there for a while, thinking and remembering what had happened last night. I really hadn't been my best. In fact, I'd pretty much been a total mess.

Finally, I decided that, yes, I could be embarrassed that I'd fallen completely apart on Slade, that I'd cried and been such a girl about the whole thing. But I wasn't embarrassed. Murders and threats didn't populate my world. It was okay that I'd been upset.

I climbed out of bed and saw my skirt and top that Slade had folded and left on the dresser. Handled just right, this could make one heck of a story at work tomorrow morning—me, Slade, an all-nighter.

No one would believe nothing happened between us, unless they saw me right now. I caught my reflection in the mirror—thick, black mascara tracks running down both cheeks.

Slade hadn't been interested last night? Go figure.

I hit the shower and left my bathroom smelling coffee. I found Slade in my kitchen. I guess I hadn't really thought he'd stay because I was surprised to see him. Seven Eleven sat beside her food bowl licking her paws and looking altogether pleased with our house guest.

"Hey," I said.

"Hey."

He'd poured coffee. I sat at the table across from him.

"Thanks for last night. I guess I screwed up your Saturday night." A memory I'd rather not recall flashed in my head. "You were hanging out with Jade last night."

Slade sipped his coffee. "Didn't happen."

It was the only good thing that had come out of the entire ordeal.

"You'd better do like that guy said, Dana, and quit poking your nose into the Sullivan murder," Slade said. "Unless you don't mind a repeat of last night."

"I'm not involved, really," I said. "I looked at mug shots but couldn't identify the guy I saw at the crime scene. I've asked a few questions, but that's all. Nothing big."

Slade shook his head. "You pissed off somebody."

Yes, it seemed I had. But who?

"Do you think they'll come after me again?" I asked.

"Maybe."

A little chill ran through me. "I don't like the idea of being scared every time I leave home," I said.

"Then don't be scared," Slade said. "Be smart."

I scrambled eggs and we finished off the coffee, then left my apartment. In the parking lot I saw my Honda sitting in my designated spot. I didn't know how Slade managed it, but I decided not to ask.

All sorts of rumors buzzed around Slade, about this past, his unexplained absences, the people he knew. When we drove away from my apartment in his Blazer, I expected to wind up at a shooting range, or at the gym for a self-defense course, or maybe a secret government installation hidden in the mountains that monitored movements of known criminals and terrorists. Instead, Slade drove to Home Depot.

He loaded a cart with all sorts of things, then drove us back to my apartment. Slade spent the afternoon fitting dowels inside my sliding windows, and installed a dead bolt lock on my door.

"Your place is as secure as I can make it unless your apartment complex okay's a surveillance system," he said, loading tools into the metal box he'd brought in from his Blazer. "Stay alert. Keep your phone close. Watch behind you when you're driving. If you think you're being tailed, go to the police station. Be cautious of strangers."

"Got it," I said.

He pulled a palm-sized canister out of his tool box and gave it to me.

"If things go sideways, use this," he said.

"Pepper spray," I realized. "Is it legal?"

He grinned. "Just don't spray a cop."

He showed me how to use it, then carried his tool box to the door.

"Thanks for everything," I said.

"It's cool," Slade said. "You need me, you call me."

He left and I closed the door, throwing the bolt on my new lock. I felt safe and secure, more in control of my world. Slade had given me good advice. He'd given me instructions, direction, something that would actually help me.

Of course, none of that would matter if Mr. Sullivan's murderer wasn't caught.

I grabbed a pad of yellow paper and a pencil from my desk in the bedroom and settled at the table in my kitchen. In the center of the page I drew a big circle and wrote Mr. Sullivan's name in it, since he was the central figure in all of this. I drew two short lines from that circle to two smaller circles and wrote Gerald Mayhew and Leonard Sullivan's named in each. I drew another line and circle, and put a question mark in it, representing the guy who'd knocked me down at the murder scene. And just because I was short on suspects, I repeated the format including Kirk Redmond's name.

I studied the lines and circles. These people were the only ones associates with the murder or the crime scene—the only ones I knew about, anyway—making them the only people who might have arranged the warning I got in the Club Vibe parking lot last night.

Gerald Mayhew had a motive—jealousy—but he also had an alibi. He'd been working; I'd verified that with his employer.

Kirk Redmond had no motive and needed no alibi. He'd simply been there on business.

Leonard Sullivan had a motive—keeping his grandfather from going to the police about something Leonard was involved in. He might have an alibi, but I'd have to find him to learn what it was.

The mystery guy who'd knocked me down was still that—a mystery.

I turned the page sideways, then upside down and studied it from different angles, trying to gain a different perspective on the names in the circles. I realized I'd left out one person—me.

I drew another line from the circle containing Mr. Sullivan's name and wrote my own name in it. I had nothing to do with the murder, yet I was involved.

From my circle, I drew another line and circle that represented the guy who'd jumped me in the Club Vibe parking lot. Another face from last night flashed in my head—Jarrod Parker. A wave of nausea washed through me.

I'd been to that club dozens of times and had never seen Jarrod. Was it a coincidence he'd been there the night I'd been accosted in the parking lot? Could he possibly have something to do with Mr. Sullvian's murder? I put Jarrod's name in a circle and drew a line to mine.

I studied the chart I'd created until the circles started to overlap. Annoyed, I realized I was getting nowhere. I locked up and left. Halfway down the staircase it occurred to me that when Slade left earlier, I hadn't watched him through the peephole, but I'd watched Nick both times he'd been to my apartment, which only annoyed me further.

I drove to my parents' house. To my delight, my mom and dad were both home, and delicious smells greeted me when I walked into the house.

"You're just in time for dinner," Mom said, as I walked into the dining room.

"What's tonight's theme?" I asked and sat down.

Mom couldn't cook a meal without a theme.

"Route 66," she said, then disappeared into the kitchen.

Dad gestured at the meatloaf, mashed potatoes, green beans and corn on the table.

"Diners across America," he explained.

Mom came in with a basket of fresh baked biscuits and sat down with us.

"Apple pie and ice cream for dessert," she announced, and we dug in.

Afterwards, Mom and I cleaned the kitchen while Dad watched TV in the family room.

"Looks like things are going better with you two," I said.

"He's taking me some place special next weekend," Mom said.

"Yeah? Where?"

She smiled. "I don't know. He won't say. Sounds very mysterious."

Sounded to me like he hadn't made definite plans yet, but I wasn't going to burst my mom's balloon. No way did I want to start hunting for a moving truck.

On the drive home I kept my gaze on my rearview mirror, as Slade had advised, watching for a car that might be following me. None did. In the driveway of my complex I checked for lurking strangers, but didn't see any, luckily, because it occurred to me that I'd left the pepper spray sitting on my kitchen counter.

When I got inside I put the pepper spray in my purse, then got ready for bed. Last night Slade had been in the bedroom with me when he was supposed to be out with Jade. She'd be so hurt, if she knew. She'd probably spent hours deciding what to wear, getting dressed, arranging for a babysitter, only to be stood up because of me.

I couldn't wait to tell her.

Chapter Twelve

When I walked into the office Monday morning, Inez's evil eye seemed to burn unusually bright, Lucas wandered around the breakroom, Carmen was already working, and Jade sat at her desk brushing her hair.

"How was your weekend?" I asked.

"It sucked," she said.

"Too much time with your kids?" I asked.

She flipped her hair at me and gave me stink-eye.

"Slade said to tell you hi," I said.

She swung her hair the other way. "Slade?"

"Yes," I said. "Your name came up over breakfast Sunday morning."

I lingered at her desk to savor her displeasure, then headed for the back of the office. My work there was done.

As I settled into my chair I realized an orange plastic pumpkin had been placed on the corner of my desk. Looking around, I saw that our office had been decorated for Halloween. Inez must have slipped in earlier than usual this morning and done it, more like an evil Grinch than a fairy godmother.

Every desk had a jack-o-lantern, the file cabinets had smiling witches perched atop them, and a dish of individually wrapped candies sat on the front counter. I was willing to bet these were the same decorations that had been here last year—and probably for at least the decade before that, thanks to Inez.

If she didn't hurry up and retire, we'd soon be able to stick her in the front window with a crow on her shoulder and straw up her sleeves.

Something to look forward to.

I saw that Carmen had left a stack of payments on my desk that she'd picked up at the post office on her way in. We usually received a lot of mail on Monday, and today proved no exception. I noted that several of my customers had sent payments, as promised, and I was relieved that their lives had turned around and they were on track again. I was anxious to tell Manny, who'd just hustled into the office carrying a briefcase and a cup of coffee, looking stressed and frowning as if he could use some good news, especially for a Monday.

The thing about good news was that it's almost always followed by bad news.

Inez rose from her desk, and called, "Attention, attention."

I kept my head down, pretending not to hear her.

"Dana, we're ready for you," she declared.

My head snapped up. "Ready? For what?"

She gave me her third-grade-teacher look.

"Now, Dana, what is it you're supposed to do this morning?"

I didn't waste precious brain cells on the matter.

"I can't solve the puzzle, Inez," I said. "Can I buy a vowel?"

Inez wasn't amused. Inez was never amused. She pursed her lips and said, "We're ready for your safety meeting."

I glanced at Manny but he ignored me. No reprieve there. I was on my own—which was okay because I already had the perfect excuse.

"No meeting today," I announced. "I have too much work to do."

"Now, Dana," she said, "Corporate's memo specifically states—"

"Not today." Manny finally came to life.

"Manny," Inez said, turning her prune-face expression to him. "Corporate has dictated that—"

"If Corporate has a problem, you tell them it was my decision," Manny told her. "They can talk to me about it."

I love that guy.

He turned to me and said, "I need you to go look at another foreclosure."

Now I wasn't loving him so much.

"The Teague account," he said, waving a print-out at me. "See what kind of shape the house is in."

I grabbed my things and left the office.

As I drove, I found myself checking my rearview mirror. No one seemed to be following me, but they may as well have, with the incident at Club Vibe still ingrained in my mind.

I wondered if I should tell Nick about it. After all, he was a detective. The guy in the parking lot was definitely tied to the murder. Maybe it would help Nick solve the case.

I fished my cell phone out of my purse and called Nick. His voice mail picked up. I left a message asking if we could meet at McDonalds near the office.

The house Manny wanted me to look at was on Ninth Street, a few blocks off of State Street. Visions of the Sullivan home flashed in my head as I parked at the curb and got out. This neighborhood wasn't quite as scary, but still, pizza places wouldn't deliver here after dark.

I glanced over the account history Manny had given me and saw that the house belonged to Janet Teague, a forty-two-year-old unmarried woman who worked at a warehouse in Hayward. She'd taken out a second mortgage with Mid-America and used the cash to pay off bills, among other things.

Rows of small frame houses sat side by side, each surrounded by a fence. As with most neighborhoods, some of the homes were well kept, others not so well. Janet's was one of the not-so-wells.

I snapped a photo of the house with my cell phone, then kept an ear out for barking dogs as I opened the gate and climbed onto the cement porch. I knocked on the front door. Nobody answered. I heard no sound from inside.

According to the comments Manny had entered on Janet's account history, things had gone well then, suddenly, she'd stopped making her payments. No call, no office visit, no explanation, no nothing.

I was annoyed with Janet which, really, wasn't like me. But Janet was the exception.

She wasn't home so I glanced around, then lifted the lid on her mailbox beside the front door and peeked inside. The electric and gas bills were there along with a Visa monthly statement, both addressed to Janet Teague, both postmarked yesterday. At least I could report to Manny that she still lived here.

It was a little early to meet Nick, but I drove to the McDonalds, backed into a spot near the entrance and waited. He pulled in ten minutes later driving a Chevy that obviously belonged to the police department, and got out of it looking as if he'd just stepped off of a magazine cover.

I sat there for a moment just watching. I wished seeing Nick didn't make my stomach feel squishy.

I wished seeing Nick didn't make me think of what he'd done to Katie Jo.

Stepping out of my car, I met him at the front fender. The sun shone in the cloudless sky but there was a little breeze, making the day cool.

Nick smiled. I didn't want to smile back, but I did.

"Hungry?" he asked, and nodded toward the restaurant.

I shook my head. "I've got to get back to work."

He didn't say anything, just waited.

"Have you gotten anywhere on the Sullivan murder?" I asked. "A suspect? A motive? Anything?"

Nick didn't answer, just continued to look at me. I saw the wheels turning in his mind, saw his cop X-ray vision switch on. On the drive over, I'd vowed not to tell Nick any more than I had to. I swore again not to crumble.

"What's up, Dana?" he asked.

I crumbled. The tone of his voice, the look on his face. Something. Something they taught at cop school. Something that demanded I spill my guts.

"I was … approached … the other night by someone connected with Mr. Sullivan's murder," I said.

Nick tensed. He shifted his weight, coming closer.

"What happened?" he asked.

"Saturday night at Club Vibe I was in the parking lot alone and a guy … a guy grabbed me and told me to stay away from Mr. Sullivan's murder."

Nick crumbled. His cool-cop demeanor vanished. His face flushed and his breathing picked up, like a bull ready to charge.

"You went into the parking lot of that club alone?" he demanded. "At night? What the hell is wrong with you, Dana? What the hell were you thinking?"

Now I got angry too.

"Did you miss the part where I said this was in connection to Mr. Sullivan's murder?" I asked. "The murder you're supposed to be solving."

"The murder you've involved yourself in?" Nick shot back. "Damnit, Dana, I told you to stay out of this."

I wasn't going to let his anger top mine. I was the injured party here.

"Never mind!" I shouted. "Forget I came here!"

Nick touched my arm. "Listen, Dana, don't you—"

"Don't tell me what to do." I jerked away from him. "I should have known better than to get involved with you—after what you did to Katie Jo Miller."

That took the color out of his face. And I was glad.

I jumped in my car and took off. I didn't know where I was going, but I was headed there in a hurry. I hit the freeway taking my anger out on the traffic, then came to my senses and slowed down after only a couple of miles.

But I was still mad. Mad at Nick. Mad at the guy who'd scared me in the parking lot. Mad at Gerald Mayhew for having an alibi, Kirk Redmond for not needing one, and Leonard Sullivan for being missing. I was mad at Mr. Sullivan for dying and leaving Mrs. Sullivan alone. I was mad at myself for not watching Slade through my peephole, and mad at Nick—again—because I'd watched him twice.

My world was a mess. I don't like messes. I decided to go back to work, back to the part of my life that was under control.

I swung by Janet Teague's house again. No change from when I was there earlier. I hoped that meant she'd found a job and was at the moment, working. Or maybe she was at the Mid-America office right now bringing her account current.

When I walked inside, Carmen sprang out of her chair.

"Guess what happened," she said. "Jarrod Parker was here."

Thank goodness. A shot of good news, for a change. He'd paid off his account to get his Mustang back thereby removing him from my life forever.

"Are you two dating?" Carmen asked.

"What?"

"He said you two were out together Saturday night," Carmen said.

"That creep," I muttered. "Did he pay off his account?"

Carmen shook her head. "He wouldn't talk to anybody but you. He said he'll come back later."

No way did I want the prospect of dealing with Jarrod Parker hanging over me all day, so I decided to take it out on Leonard Sullivan.

I pulled every file folder of every loan Leonard, his grandparents, his aunts, uncles and cousins had ever had with us and went through them with a fine-toothed comb. I phoned every previous job, every relative, every friend listed. No one, absolutely no one, had seen or heard from Leonard. I pulled a new credit report on him hoping I'd discover his new address or employer. Nada. Leonard was not to be found.

I sat at my desk with my telephone up to my ear, staring at the computer screen so it would look as if I were working. Nick popped into my head and I recalled how, back in high school, he'd seemed genuinely interested in Katie Jo—so much so that I'd actually been a bit jealous of their relationship. She was crazy about him. They'd seemed perfect for each other. Then, everything had turned out so badly—for Katie Jo, anyway.

My mom and dad floated into my head. All of those years of marriage, of problems, of dealing with money matters, kids, holidays, relatives, only to have it all threatened by a television sports package. Unlike Nick and Katie Jo, things between my folks seemed to have deteriorated slowly until one day—boom—Mom had taken all she was going to take.

I guess the outcome of any relationship couldn't be predicted. Arthur and Gladys Sullivan had probably worked extremely hard when Leonard had been growing up. They'd taken him in, given in a home, taken care of him when he was sick, helped with homework, gone to school plays, and done everything they knew to do to give him a good life.

I doubted either of them would have predicted that Leonard would turn his back on the family at a time when Mrs. Sullivan needed him the most. And all because of that argument she'd said Leonard had with his grandfather. Could their relationship have ended in the blink of an eye? Or had it been crumbling for years?

Either way, I was going to find Leonard. I'd see to it that he visited his grandmother, that he did the right thing by Mr. Sullivan—no matter what it took. And I wasn't listening to any excuses Leonard might have. Under the circumstances, I couldn't imagine an explanation he could have for his actions.

A chill rushed through me as other possibilities flashed in my head.

Maybe Leonard wasn't simply ignoring his grandmother.

Maybe he was hiding.

Or, maybe, he was dead.

CHAPTER THIRTEEN

Manny and I worked late. It was kind of nice with just the two of us in the office—no customers, no Inez, no hair flipping. We walked to the darkened parking lot together, then parted ways. There were a lot of things I could have done with what was left of the evening, lots more that I *should* have done. Instead, I did something I shouldn't.

I accessed the address of the Stanford Medical Clinic on my cell phone, punched it into my GPS, and headed for Dayton Avenue. I found the clinic easily and pulled into a parking space at the rear of the building.

Gerald Mayhew had told me he was working here the night Mr. Sullivan was murdered. I'd verified with his employer that he did, in fact, work here. Still, I wanted to see for myself.

It was after seven now and Mayhew should be on duty, unless this happened to be his night off. I sat in my car for about fifteen minutes before I saw a uniformed guard come around the corner of the building on foot. The security lighting wasn't great but I could see right away that this wasn't Mayhew. This guy looked about 23 years old, thin, white, and bored.

It must be tough for security firms to get people willing to spend an eight- hour shift pacing the perimeter of a building, especially on the evening and night shifts. I suppose that was how they ended up with old men like Gerald Mayhew and this young guy on their payroll.

Scrounging through my purse, I found my pepper spray and slipped it into the pocket of my jacket. I scanned the parking lot looking for anything suspicious—not that I knew what *suspicious* looked like, really, but I checked anyway.

I headed toward the guard. He saw me and walked over.

"Where's Gerald?" I asked, craning my neck as if I expected him to walk up and join us.

The guy rested his hands on his big leather belt. "Just me on duty."

I frowned, hoping I looked puzzled, and said, "Doesn't Gerald work evenings?"

He didn't seem surprised that I'd asked. I suppose he was glad to have somebody to talk to.

"It's his regular shift, but he called off again tonight," he said. "More hours for me."

"We all need the work when we can get it," I agreed. "But it must tick you off, sometimes. I mean, you've got a life too. You can't just drop everything and cover someone else's shift."

"Yeah, like last week," the guard said. "I had Lakers tickets and I couldn't go because of Mayhew."

I remembered that a basketball game had been on television the evening a week ago when I'd walked into the Sullivan living room.

"You missed the Lakers?" I asked. "Last Monday night's game?"

"Yeah," the guy grumbled. "I had to give the tickets to my brother-in-law."

"That's criminal," I told him.

"Tell me about it."

I glanced around for no particular reason, then said, "I'll catch Gerald another time."

His expression showed a little suspicion. "What do you want Mayhew for?"

Good question. Luckily, I had a good answer.

"My mom is having one of those home decorating parties," I said, "and she wants Gerald's wife to come, but she can't come, so I was supposed to leave a sales brochure with Gerald to give to Ida so she can look it over and order something."

As I'd hoped, the guy had tuned out halfway through my explanation.

"Can I leave the brochure with you?" I asked, pointing to my car.

He shook his head. "I don't know when I'll see Mayhew again."

"Okay," I said. "Well, good night."

I got into my car and left.

So much for Gerald Mayhew's alibi.

I mentally kicked myself for not thinking sooner about checking his alibi at his actual work site. A detective, a trained professional, would have. But I was neither, and at least I'd thought of it—finally.

I'm a quick study, so I decided that digging a little deeper into some other aspects of Mr. Sullivan's murder would be a good idea.

I whipped into a parking lot and accessed the Internet for Kirk

Redmond's building contractor Web site. I loaded the address of his business into my GPS and started driving again.

A short fifteen minutes later, I reached his location. It was housed in an industrial strip mall sandwiched between an auto parts store and an electronics repair shop. Each unit had an office attached to a small warehouse with a roll-up door. Some of the units had no business name printed on the door, yet they looked occupied. I wondered what sort of *business* went on there.

Kirk Redmond's name was printed prominently on the front of the unit his business occupied, along with his contractor's license number and hours of operation. Through the glass door a feeble security light burned, and I saw a stack of paint cans and a couple of ladders. Nothing looked out of the ordinary.

I sat in my car for a couple of minutes, staring at Redmond's business and thinking.

He had no known motive for murdering Mr. Sullivan. Plus, he had a legitimate reason for being at the house, even if it was a bit odd that the Sullivans wanted their house painted when they couldn't pay their bills.

I was forced to mark Kirk Redmond's name off of my mental list of suspects. That left me with Gerald Mayhew, whose alibi had been blown, and Leonard Sullivan, who may have a great alibi, for all I knew.

Of course, it was possible the police had already solved the murder, arrested a suspect and closed the case.

That thought caused Nick Travis to pop into my head.

I pushed him out, and drove to my parents' house.

They were both watching television when I arrived. Dad managed to wave without taking his eyes off the screen as Mom and I went into the kitchen.

"What's wrong?" she asked, and gave me her mom-look. "Something's wrong, Dana. What is it?"

I hadn't told her about my involvement with the Sullivan case, so I sure as heck wasn't going to mention what I'd been doing tonight.

"I'm concerned about you and Dad," I said, which was the truth—part of it, anyway. "How are things going with you two?"

"Just fine," Mom said. "Are you hungry? I've got roast beef, potatoes and carrots."

"Crock Pot week, huh?"

She smiled and nodded.

"Sounds good," I said. "Has Dad told you any more about your plans for this weekend?"

Mom grinned as she placed my dinner in the microwave.

"It's still a big mystery," she said. "I'm getting excited."

And I was getting anxious. Dad better have something big up his sleeve that was worthy of all this buildup.

Mom and I sat at the kitchen table while I ate, and she filled me in on her day.

"Something else is bothering you," Mom said, as I got up to rinse my plate.

I realized then that the knot I'd had in my belly for hours was from the look on Nick's face standing outside McDonald's when I'd brought up Katie Jo Miller. I'd shocked him and, at the time, I'd been glad. Now, looking back, I didn't feel so great about it.

"I was thinking about Katie Jo Miller," I said. "You remember, from high school?"

"Of course I remember," Mom said. "What a terrible ordeal she went through."

"Do you remember much about Nick Travis?" I asked.

"A little," she said. "I remember you had a crush on him."

"I did," I admitted. "But not after what he did to Katie Jo."

"Yes, there was that rumor," Mom said. She rose from the table and opened the dishwasher. "You know, there was something odd about that family."

"I didn't know Nick's family," I said.

"No, not Nick's family," Mom said. "Katie Jo's family."

"Katie Jo's family?" I echoed. "Mom, she was my best friend."

"I know, and I always liked her." She shook her head. "But that family of hers. Something wasn't right about them. That's why I never let you sleep over there."

I'd forgotten that. Back in high school, I'd never slept at Katie Joe's house but she'd been to our home many times. I hadn't given it any thought back then.

"What was wrong with them?" I asked.

"I don't know, exactly," Mom said. "It was just a feeling I had."

On that note, I left. I drove home thinking about my pepper spray and watching my rearview mirror. No one seemed to be following me. In the parking lot of my complex, I saw no suspicious characters.

Seven Eleven greeted me as I flipped on lights, threw the dead bolt, and dropped my purse on the table. I gave her a can of cat food, then changed into sweats and called Jillian; my day hadn't been the greatest and talking to my best friend seemed comforting. Her voice mail picked up. I left a message.

I wasn't tired enough to sleep and TV didn't seem appealing. I fetched the yellow legal pad I'd left beside my computer and dropped onto the sofa in my living room.

I looked at the circles and the names I'd written in them. I scratched out Kirk Redmond's name, then drew another circle around Gerald Mayhew's name. Not only did Mayhew have a motive, but he'd lied about having an alibi. Why would he do that?

A few thoughts ran through my head and I realized there were several reasons he might lie about being at work. Maybe he was cheating on his wife, or maybe he was out scoring weed—or maybe he really had murdered Mr. Sullivan.

I looked at Leonard Sullivan's name and wished I could mark through it. I couldn't because I hadn't found him. I'd made no progress whatsoever in locating him.

Irritated, I tossed the tablet aside and got ready for bed.

I stared at the ceiling of my bedroom and realized that something more than murder suspects and alibis had been bugging me all afternoon.

Nick hadn't called.

After blasting him in the McDonald's parking lot with his and Katie Jo's past, I'd expected him to call and explain. Explain what, I didn't know, exactly. An apology? An admission that he was, and still is, the biggest jerk who ever walked upright? Offer a defense of what had happened back in high school?

Lying there in the dark, my heart got a little heavier.

Not only had Nick not called to explain, he hadn't called at all.

* * *

When I arrived at work the next morning, Carmen wasn't at the front counter.

"Her daughter is sick," Inez explained. "She'll be in later."

I didn't want to wait for Carmen to show up to get the payments from the post office. I needed to know which customers had paid so I could get down to work. Still, I wasn't anxious to venture out on my own.

Manny wasn't in yet. I considered taking Lucas along but couldn't picture him having my back in a fight. That left Inez and Jade.

While I had absolutely no compunction about pushing either of them out in front of me if something went down, I decided to take Jade simply because she had the widest butt and would offer the best cover.

I grabbed my keys from my purse, waited until Inez picked up the telephone, then rushed to Jade's desk.

"Come on," I said. "You're going to the post office with me."

She rolled her eyes. "Why would I want to go to the post office with you?"

"Because it's a good excuse to get out of the office," I said. "Let's go."

When we reached the door I turned back and called, "We're going to the post office, Inez," then rushed out before she could respond.

Jade had on a short skirt with a slit up her thigh, a silk blouse with the top two buttons open, and stilettos with four inch heels. Not the best outfit for walking to the post office, but we did get two honks and a whistle from the homeless guy on the corner.

We climbed the concrete steps with Jade teetering on her spike heels, and went inside.

"Ours is back here," I said, as I led the way into one of the alcoves lined with post office boxes.

I opened our box and saw that it was stuffed full. What a great way to start my day knowing that so many of my customers were doing well enough to send in their payments.

Some of the envelopes were wedged inside so that I had to struggle to pull them all out. Right away I recognized the names of several customers who'd been having a really tough time.

Maybe Jade had brought me good luck, I thought. Maybe having her for backup had paid off. Maybe—

A hand caught my arm and spun me around. I slammed backwards into the bank of post office boxes. Standing over me was the same guy who'd grabbed me outside Club Vibe.

CHAPTER FOURTEEN

Or maybe it wasn't the same guy. I don't know. Tall, knit cap, sunglasses. My heard pounded so hard I heard it in my ears—no way could I make sense of anything.

"I told you once, bitch," he said, leaving down.

I dropped the envelopes. They spilled out of my hand and littered the floor around us.

"You keep your damn nose out of Sullivan's business," he said. "Or *else.*"

He spun around and left.

My knees shook. My thoughts raced. My pepper spray? My cell phone? Where were they?

The office, I realized, I'd left them in the office because I'd come here with Jade thinking—

Jade? Where the heck was Jade?

I staggered out of the alcove and saw her butt sticking out as she leaned over the half-door, talking to the postal worked inside. My fear turned to rage.

"Jade!" I screamed. "What are you *doing*?"

She spared me a glance, gave me a hair flip, and turned away.

It was more than I could stand. I headed for the door, then remembered the payments. I gathered them up, then thrust them at Jade.

"Take these back to the office!"

I threw open the door and dashed down the concrete steps. I wasn't scared anymore, I was boiling mad. I hoped that guy would show his face again—so I could rip it off his head.

Somebody was going to pay the price for me being frightened out of my wits again, and that somebody was Nick Travis.

I jumped into my car in the office parking and drove to the police station. I didn't wait to be acknowledged by the officer on duty. I straight-armed the door and marched to the squad room. Nick sat at his desk.

"You idiot!" I screamed.

Nick looked up—along with a dozen other men.

I stomped over to his desk, glaring down at him.

"You are a waste of skin!" I shouted. "You're the worst detective on the planet!"

Nick sprang to his feet. I liked it better glaring down at him, but I had no intention of stopping.

"While you're in here sitting on your butt," I said, and pointed toward the building entrance, "I'm out there being accosted *again*."

Nick frowned and opened his mouth to speak, but I cut him off.

"Maybe if you got up and moved around a little, you'd solve the Sullivan case—or at least make some progress!" I yelled. "Maybe then the streets would be safe for decent people to get their mail!"

"What happened?"

Nick's voice was so forceful I had to answer.

I flung out both arms. "I was attacked at the post office!"

Nick hustled me into one of the interview rooms off to the side. He sat me in one of the chairs that surrounded a little table, and closed the door.

I sprang to my feet. "I don't want to sit down!"

"Tell me what happened," Nick said, sounding way too calm to suit me. "Are you hurt?"

"He grabbed my arm," I said. "I probably have AIDS, or cooties, or something."

Nick just looked at me in that reasonable way of his, making me calm down.

Suddenly, I was exhausted. All that emotion had taken its toll. I plopped into a chair.

Nick sat down next to me and waited a few minutes while I caught my breath.

"Now," he said softly. "Tell me what happened."

I explained what had just occurred at the post office.

"Was it the same man you saw at Club Vibe?" he asked.

"I don't know," I said, angry with myself because I wasn't sure. "He just told me to stay away from Mr. Sullivan's murder, that's all I know for sure."

Nick huffed. "Dana, I told you to steer clear of this investigation."

My anger flared again.

"This is your fault," I told him. "Don't sit there and act like it isn't."

Nick eased back a little. "My fault?"

"If you told me what was going on with Mr. Sullivan's murder when I asked, I wouldn't have to check into things on my own," I told him. "So don't sit there now and pretend you didn't have a hand in this."

Nick just looked at me.

"And, obviously, I have done a better job investigation this case than you have," I pointed out, "since I've had two death threats and you haven't had a single one."

I paused, a little troubled, and said, "You haven't had any death threats, have you?"

"Not a one," he said.

"Okay, then, there you go," I said, and sat back in my chair.

Nick heaved a weary sign. "How about we have a mutual exchange of information?"

I managed to look smug and self-righteous for a few seconds, then finally relented.

"All right," I said. "You first."

"To be honest with you, Dana," he said, and sat forward resting his elbows on the table, "I haven't made much progress in the Sullivan case. Nobody's talking. Not the family, the neighbors, nobody. There is no motive, no real suspects. Plus, I've had three more homicides since Sullivan's."

This didn't seem like much of a mutual exchange of information because Nick didn't have any info to exchange. I wondered if he was really telling me the truth, but I had no way of knowing for sure, and we wouldn't get anywhere if I didn't give him something in return.

"Have you checked into Gerald Mayhew?" I asked.

"Who's he?" Nick asked.

I wasn't surprised that he hadn't heard about Mayhew. I'd gotten the information only because of my connection with the family. I explained about Mayhew's jealous nature and the suspected affair between his wife and Mr. Sullivan, and how he'd lied about his alibi.

"Also," I said, "I questioned Mayhew last week, then was jumped at Club Vibe. Last night I was at his job asking for him, and this morning the post office thing happened."

Nick pulled a little tablet from the pocket of his jacket and wrote down everything I'd told him.

"I'll check into it," he said. "Anything else?"

I considered telling him about Leonard's disappearance and my questioning the timing of Mr. Sullivan wanting his house painted, but I'd given him enough information for now.

"Nothing else," I said.

"I'll take it from here." Nick pointed his finger at me. "You back off."

I didn't promise that I would, because I didn't want to give him the satisfaction.

"You'll let me know?" I asked, gesturing to his little tablet.

"I'll keep you informed," he promised.

We sat there for another minute or so looking at each other. I wondered if he'd take this opportunity to explain about Katie Jo. I wondered if he even remembered that I'd brought it up yesterday.

Apparently not. Nick rose from his chair, my cue to leave, then he surprised me by saying, "Do you want me to take you home?"

Okay, I'd barged into the police station shrieking at the top of my lungs, but that was in a moment of passion. I'd cooled off now. Besides, I didn't want to be coddled—not by Nick. Not with that whole Katie Jo thing between us.

"I'm going to work," I said, and left.

Manny was on the phone when I walked into the office. He gave me a look when I passed his desk and I figured he wanted to know where I'd been. No doubt Inez had started her stop-watch the minute Jade returned from the post office without me.

Just as I settled into my desk, Carmen brought me a phone message.

"She thought you'd like to go," Carmen said.

I read the message. It was from Leona Wiley advising me that Mr. Sullivan's graveside service was today.

When Manny got off the phone I sat down in the chair beside his desk.

"What's up, Dana?" he asked. "You okay?"

I didn't want to go into what had happened at the post office, so I just waved my hands around a bit and said, "I'm having some issues right now."

"Need anything?" Manny asked.

"No," I said.

He looked relieved, and I couldn't blame him.

"I'd like to go to Mr. Sullivan's funeral today," I said.

"Sure," he said. "Want some company?"

I shook my head. "I'll be okay by myself."

I went back to my desk. The more I considered his suggestion, the better it sounded. Some company would help.

I dug out my cell phone and called Slade.

"Will you go to a funeral with me today?" I asked.

"Cool."

* * *

Mr. Sullivan's service was on State Street. A long row of parked cars lined the road that wound through the cemetery. I eased my Honda in line with the others, and got out.

The day was sunny and warm, perfect Southern California weather. Too pretty a day to spend at the cemetery.

But here I was, and maybe it was good that I was here. Saying good-bye to sweet old Mr. Sullivan might be what I needed. Closure, and all that other psycho-babble.

I spotted Slade leaning against his Blazer farther up the procession line. Mr. Ex-Special Ops had transformed into Mr. GQ. He wore a dark suit, white shirt, and gray tie. Very sharp.

We walked to the folding chairs that had been set up under the green canopy covering Mr. Sullivan's casket. Mrs. Sullivan and Leona Wiley sat in chairs, surrounded by a couple dozen family members. Friends crowded at the rear of the chairs, everyone dressed in dark colors.

Mrs. Sullivan seemed to have shrunk since I'd seen her sitting in her living room with Mr. Sullivan, watching her stories. Back before her life had been turned upside down.

Slade and I kept to the rear of the gathering as the minister conducted the service, and I was touched by all the sad faces around me. I thought about how short life really was, of that brief window of time we're given to accomplish something, help somebody, improve the world.

I projected myself into the future. One day I'd be standing at my parents' funerals. One day, my kids would be standing at mine.

I didn't like either scenario.

Another thought came to me as the minister offered a prayer. If things had gone differently Saturday night in the parking lot of Club Vibe, or at the post office this morning, my parents could have been attending my funeral.

Fear whipped through me.

What was it like to die? To simply cease to exist? I couldn't fathom the emptiness—or the fulfillment of Heaven. All I knew was that I didn't want to miss out on my life.

Maybe Nick was right about me backing off.

When the service ended, Slade and I approached Mrs. Sullivan and I expressed my sympathy. She looked dazed, lost. Slade took her hand and leaned down, speaking softly to her.

"Thank you for coming," Leona said.

"It was a nice service," I said, because I didn't know what else to say.

She gazed at the people gathered in little knots, talking quietly.

"A nice turn out. Real nice," she said. A different sadness clouded her face as she turned back to me. "I guess you didn't have any luck finding Leonard."

I felt as if she'd slapped me. In fact, if she'd hit me it would have hurt less.

"I've not heard a word from that boy, not a single word. Nobody has," Mrs. Wiley said. "It's a shame, just a shame. Gladys is so disappointed. What in the world could he be thinking?"

I didn't know. But I was getting a really bad feeling about Leonard.

Gazing from Mrs. Wiley to Mrs. Sullivan, to all the other faces of family and friends, I knew I couldn't back off. No matter what Nick said. No matter what.

"I'll keep looking for Leonard," I promised, and fought the urge to draw a little "X" over my heart. "But in the meantime, is there anything else I can do? Anything at all?"

I hoped she'd name something—anything—and give me a chance to redeem myself. I'd been a total failure so far.

"Oh, no, honey," Mrs. Wiley said. "You've done enough."

"There must be something," I insisted.

She paused for a few seconds, then said, "Well, there is one thing."

I felt like a puppy waiting for a treat.

"Could you come by my place tomorrow around noon?" Mrs. Wiley asked. "I can't drive and Gladys, well, she's in no shape to get behind the wheel."

"Sure," I said quickly. "I can come over on my lunch hour."

"Thank you, honey," Mrs. Wiley said.

I felt as if a lead weight had been lifted from my shoulders. Finally, something I could do—that I could actually accomplish.

I spotted Slade standing in the center of a half dozen elderly black ladies, all in hats and holding large purses. The women chattered and Slade nodded, looking at them earnestly and, apparently, holding up his end of the conversation.

It was weird—but this had been a weird day.

When the crowd around Slade finally broke up, he walked over to me.

"Thanks for coming," I said.

"It's cool," he said.

We parted ways, me going back to the office, him going who-knows-where.

Manny wiggled his fingers at me when I walked in, and I sat down beside his desk.

"You're not going to believe this," he said. "Sean and Belinda

Griffin's house burned down."

My mouth flew open.

"I got a call from Belinda," Manny said. "It happened Sunday night. The whole place went up."

The pretty little Victorian home out in Webster that I'd done the foreclosure look-up on last week flashed in my head.

"Were they home?" I asked. "Are they okay?"

"Visiting her mother in Laughlin at the time, according to Belinda," Manny said. "They're back in town now staying with friends."

I sat there for a couple of minutes, soaking it in.

"I hate to say this, but the fire solves a lot of their problems," I said.

"Sure does," Manny agreed.

Manny and I looked at each other and I knew we were thinking the same thing—was the timing of the fire a little too convenient?

"What happens now?" I asked. "About their account, I mean."

"We'll hold off on the foreclosure until we hear from their insurance agent," he said.

I went back to my desk and tried to work, but I couldn't stop thinking about the Griffins. They'd lost their house and everything in it, but after the way Belinda had acted the last time we talked, I wondered if it made any difference to her.

Yet another black cloud descended when Jarrod Parker walked into the office. I wasn't in the mood to deal with him, but I wanted his account to disappear—and him along with it.

Looking at him standing at the front counter, I flashed on how I'd connected him to the guy who'd jumped me in the parking lot last Saturday night. Now, my best guess was that Gerald Mayhew had been behind the incident. Yet, somehow, I couldn't forget that Jarrod had been there that night, too.

Carmen seated him in one of the small interview rooms off the main office. I printed his account summary and went inside.

"Hi, Dana," Jarrod said, smiling up at me.

I dropped into the chair across the table from him.

"You'd better be here to pay off your account," I told him.

I knew I wasn't being nice to Jarrod—and I'm always nice to my customers. But this guy didn't deserve my kindness or my patience.

He folded his hands and leaned closer. "Yeah, Dana, but I need to find out how much I owe."

This was a lame excuse for interrupting my day because I'd already given him that info when Slade and I repo'd his car—plus the amount was printed on his monthly statement.

"It's the same figure you already have," I told him.

"Well, huh, Dana, I don't remember how much it is." He gave me a lazy grin, which I'm sure he thought was charming. "Guess I've just had other things on my mind."

I went back to my desk, accessed his account on my computer, printed the balance, then went back into the interview room and slapped it down on the table in front of him.

"You've got ten days—by law—to pay off your account," I said, "or your Mustang will belong to someone else."

He grinned again. "You're one tough chick, Dana."

I thought I was going to barf across the table on him. I almost wished I could.

"So," Jarrod said, sitting back. "What're you doing this weekend?"

I rose from my chair. "Look, Jarrod, I don't want to see you in this office again unless you've got the cash to pay off your account. Understand?"

He looked me up and down and said, "You like me, don't you?"

I stomped out of the room.

Could this day get any worse?

CHAPTER FIFTEEN

I decided a free meal might perk up my day considerably, so after work I headed over to my parents' house. Crock Pot Week continued with a chicken and wild rice concoction.

"So, how was your day?" Mom asked as we sat down to eat.

I didn't want to tell her about the funeral so I went with my tamest story of the day.

"One of my customer's house burned down," I said.

"Oh, dear," Mom said. "Was anybody hurt?"

"No one was home," I said.

"That fire out in Webster?" Dad asked. "Saw it in the newspaper. Didn't know you had such shady customers."

Mom looked slightly alarmed. "What do you mean?"

"The fire's being called suspicious," Dad said. "The arson investigators are crawling all over it."

"No kidding," I said. Odd that Belinda hadn't mentioned that little bit of info when she called Manny today.

"I don't like the sound of that," Mom said.

I sensed her maybe-you-should-move-back-home speech coming so I distracted her.

"I need boots for my Halloween costume," I said. "Want to come shopping with me, Mom?"

"Tonight?" She shook her head. "I've got the Ladies Auxiliary meeting at church."

We cleared the table, and Mom and I did the dishes while Dad sat in front of the television.

"Have you found out what Dad's big plan is for the weekend?" I asked.

"We're going to a party," Mom announced.

This, I hadn't expected.

"Dad knows somebody who's having a party?" I asked.

Whenever I heard Dad together with his friends, they discussed things like radial tires and lawn fertilizer. My dad did not run with the party crowd.

"A party?" I asked. "Are you sure?"

"Oh, yes," Mom said. "It should be fun."

"Well, okay," I said. "You'll need a costume. Why don't you and I—"

"It's not a costume party," Mom said.

"It's Halloween weekend," I said. "Everybody will be wearing a costume."

"This isn't the sort of party you and your friends go to," Mom said. "No costumes. I had your dad check twice."

"Well, okay, if you're sure," I said. "Do you know anybody else who's going?"

"No, but your dad does," Mom said. "That's the nicest part. We can make new friends."

"Then we should at least get you something new to wear," I said.

Mom shook her head. "Not necessary. I have dozens of dresses in my closet."

"But don't you want something new?" I asked.

"No, no. I have a favorite dress I want to wear," Mom said. "I should take a hostess gift. I think a mum plant would do nicely."

It wasn't my idea of a great evening, but Mom was excited and that was good enough for me.

"A mum plant sounds perfect," I said.

After we finished with the kitchen I phoned Jillian. She was up for a trip to the mall. I picked her up and we hit the stores. She didn't really need anything but that didn't stop her from buying a terrific pair of jeans and two T-shirts.

By the time we got to the third shoe store and I hadn't found the kind of boots I wanted for my pirate costume, I was ready to call it a night. Then Jillian's shoe-sale alarm went off.

"Oh, my God. Look!" She pointed across the mall like one of those hunting dogs. "There they are!"

I followed her to the shop window and peered at the boots she was salivating over.

"You've got to try them on, Dana," Jillian declared, and pulled me into the store.

The clerk seemed to think the boots—thigh-high, black leather with four-inch heels—were a great idea too, as he watched me pull them on. I walked to the mirror.

"I look like a hooker," I said.

"Slightly slutty," Jillian said. "They're perfect for your costume."

I looked at the end of the box and said, "These things cost a fortune."

"This is Felderman's party we're going to, Dana," Jillian said. "Everybody will be there. You *have* to get these boots."

That was a good enough reason for me. I whipped out my Visa and signed away just over a hundred bucks.

I knew that was a lot of money to spend on boots for a Halloween costume, but in a few years I'd be showing up at parties with mum plants. I decided I should live large while I could.

By the time I dropped Jillian off at her place, I was ready to fall into bed. I drove home, parked, wrestled the big box of boots out of my trunk and headed for my apartment.

A man stepped out of the shadows. I screamed, threw the boot box at him, and ran.

My heart pounded as I raced for my car. My pepper spray! My phone! Oh, God, why hadn't I looked around before I left my car? Where were my keys?

"Dana! Hold up!"

A man appeared alongside me. It was Nick, my boot box tucked under his arm.

I stopped, panting. "You scared ten years off of my life!"

"I came by to see if you were all right," he said.

Annoyed, I yanked the box away from him.

"What have you got in there?" Nick asked.

I took a couple of deep breaths. "They're for my Halloween costume."

He lifted the lid from the box.

"Not going as the French maid this year, I see. Or are you?" He grinned, then looked serious. "I didn't mean to scare you. Sorry."

His apology and that grin of his tapped off most of my anger.

"Just don't sneak up on me again," I said. "I'm kind of punchy these days."

He nodded toward my apartment building. "I left you something outside your door. Something chocolate."

Nick knew me way too well now. That should have bothered me, but didn't.

"Want to come up? I asked.

Nick glanced at his wristwatch, and I saw that he looked tired, maybe a little frazzled. His collar stood open, his tie pulled loose.

I guess I wasn't the only one who could have a bad day.

"I've got beer in the fridge," I offered.

He hesitated a few seconds, then nodded. "I have something to tell you."

He took my boot box and we walked upstairs together. Outside my door I found a quart of chocolate fudge ice cream in an insulated bag.

Seven Eleven came running when we walked inside and I flipped on the lights. She rubbed her head against my leg while I dumped food into her bowl.

When I turned I saw Nick holding up one of my new boots and looking at my legs.

"If this isn't part of a French maid costume," he said, "it would be a crime."

He grinned and my stomach quivered. I distracted myself by getting Nick a beer from the fridg. I considered taking one for myself, but decided I'd better go with the chocolate fudge ice cream.

Nick took off his sport coat and shoulder holster, and dropped into a chair at my kitchen table. I got a spoon, pried off the lid of the ice cream container, and sat down.

"Rough day?" I asked.

He tipped up his beer. "A double murder in Jackson Park."

I cringed. "That's rough, all right."

"A couple of gang bangers. We have a suspect. Recovered a small arsenal of weapons." Nick managed a small smile. "Sometimes we get lucky."

"I don't suppose this was connected to Mr. Sullivan's murder?" I asked.

"No connection," he said. "I checked out your Gerald Mayhew. You're right. He wasn't at work the night of the murder."

"Where was he?" I asked.

"We haven't found him yet to ask him," Nick said.

Somebody else was missing, in addition to Leonard Sullivan?

"You don't think Mayhew's dead, do you?" I asked.

He looked puzzled. "Why would you ask that?"

"I've got death on the brain lately, l guess," I said.

We were quiet for a few minutes while Nick drank his beer, I ate ice cream, and Seven Eleven crunched her dry food. Finally, Nick set his bottle aside.

"You were friends with Katie Jo back in high school, weren't you?" he asked.

My gaze bobbed from my bowl to Nick's face. He'd caught me off guard with that question.

"Katie Jo was my best friend," I said.

Nick grinned. "You were a hell-raiser back then."

"I was not," I insisted. "I was a nice girl."

"I remember," he told me. "You didn't take crap from anybody."

"Well, okay, maybe my people skills weren't the best," I said. "But I've improved since then."

Nick raised an eyebrow.

"I have," I told him.

He shook his head. "That's one of the things I like about you, Dana. Don't apologize for it."

Nick Travis was so darned handsome. He made my heart pump a little faster and my stomach feel gooey. There were definitely signs of something between us—something I didn't want to put a name to, something I didn't dare act on with Katie Jo in our mutual history.

"Why are you bringing up Katie Jo?" I asked.

He looked at me for a long while, then pulled on the back of his neck.

"Did she tell you about … what happened?" he asked.

"You mean about how you got her pregnant, made her have an abortion, then dumped her and left town?" I asked.

Nick just stared at me as if he were hurt, or disappointed. Or maybe embarrassed.

"Is that what you think happened?" he asked.

"Is there something else I should know?" I countered.

Nick paused for a moment, then drained his beer and put on his gun and jacket.

"I've got to go," he said.

I followed him to the door and he stood in the hallway looking at me as if there were something he wanted to ask, something he wanted to say. Or, maybe, something he wanted me to say.

Finally, he left.

I closed the door, threw the security bolt and forced myself not to look out the peephole. I had a sinking feeling I'd missed something just now.

Darn my poor people skills. If I'd known what to say, I might have drawn Nick out. I might have gotten him to tell me whatever it was he'd seemed to want to say to me.

Maybe he would have told me he was sorry for what he'd done to Katie Jo, and that big wedge between us would have vanished.

Or maybe he would have said that he wasn't sorry, and that big wedge would have dug in deeper.

Or maybe he would have told me the rumors were wrong. He wasn't the one responsible for what happened to Katie Jo.

Or maybe I could run down to the parking lot right now and tell him that the whole thing happened a long time ago, we'd both changed, and I'd just forget about it.

Except I couldn't forget about it.

I scooped up Seven Eleven, turned off the lights and went to bed.

CHAPTER SIXTEEN

Sitting at my desk the next morning, flipping through the payments Carmen had just brought back from the post office, I knew my day was going to be great. Lots of customers had paid, even several whom I knew had been having really bad financial difficulties. Good to know things had turned around for them.

Then, things turned around for me.

"Dana," Manny called from his desk.

I glanced over and saw him scowling at his computer. Not a good sign. I definitely did not want to go check out another house that might get foreclosed on.

"Dana?" Carmen called from the front of the office. "You have a call on line two. It's Jarrod Parker."

Oh, so early on a Wednesday morning to be caught between two evils—getting assigned a crappy duty from my boss, or talking to an idiot.

Still, my choice was easy.

I grabbed the phone. "What do you want, Jarrod?" I asked.

"Hello, Dana," he said, oblivious to my ill-mannered greeting. "How're you doing?"

He had that little *tone* in his voice. What was with this guy? It made me all the more suspicious of him.

"I was wondering, Dana," he said, "how long after I pay off that account can I pick up my car?"

"You've got the cash to pay it off?" I asked.

"Well, yeah ... sort of."

I knew what that *really* meant.

"I'll release the car as soon as you pay off your account," I told him.

"That's cool," he said. "Look, I'm coming over that way today. Want to have lunch, or something?"

If I'd had any sort of appetite before, it was gone now.

"All I want from you is your account paid off," I said.

"Okay, so, what time should I pick you up?" Jarrod asked.

"Never!" I gripped the phone tighter and pulled in a deep breath. "Just pay off your account, Jarrod. That's all I want from you."

"I'll be there as quick as I can," he promised.

"Fine," I said, and hung up.

As badly as I wanted Jarrod Parker's account to be paid off and disappear from my life forever, I considered it might be worth it to just sell his car and be rid of him once and for all.

I came to my senses when Manny called my name again. I plopped down in the chair beside his desk.

"What's the story with the Parker repo?" he asked. "I've got a meeting with the DM today. What should I tell him?"

The District Manager wouldn't be interested in hearing what a jerk Jarrod Parker was, so I had to come up with something that would keep him happy for a while.

"He'll redeem his car by the end of the week," I said, and knew I was being a little more than slightly optimistic.

"That's what I like to hear," Manny said.

I went back to my desk and spent the morning trying to accomplish tasks that Mid-America was paying me for. At noon, I ate the sandwich I'd brought with me, then left the office.

Yesterday at the funeral I'd promised Leona Wiley I'd come by her house and drive her somewhere—the grocery store, probably—so I headed to Devon. When I cruised past the Sullivan house I noticed the crime scene tape had disappeared and the makeshift shrine of candles and flowers out front was gone. Poof. Just like that. Evidence of the destroyed lives had disappeared. But maybe it was just as well. Maybe it was time to move on.

I circled the block to Leona Wiley's place, parked at the curb and knocked on the door. She opened it right away wearing a maroon dress and hat, which seemed an odd outfit for a trip to the grocery store, but okay.

"You're so sweet to do this, honey," Leona said, stepping out onto the porch and pulling the door closed.

I leaned around her, peering into the disappearing living room.

"Is Mrs. Sullivan coming with us?" I asked.

"Oh, no. I told her it would do her good, but she isn't up to it yet," Leona said, and shook her head. "Besides, she doesn't really have the

money to spend on something like this. Not yet, anyway. We'll have to
see how things go."

"Do you mean with her finances?" I asked.

"Gladys is worried about how she's going to make ends meet, now
that Arthur is gone," Leona said. "They didn't have much, you know,
just the house."

I remembered from the Sullivans' loan application that they still had a
mortgage on their home. They'd refinanced it several times over the
years using the cash for home improvements, paying off other bills, and
medical expenses. Their budget had been tight, even when Mr. Sullivan
was alive and working his part-time job. I didn't know how Gladys
would make it now without help from somewhere.

Leonard sprang into my mind. Where was he when his grandmother
needed him?

"She'll probably sell the house," Leona said. "I told her she could
live here with me. It's kind of lonely for me, since my Edgar passed
three years ago. Gladys and I always get along. Some sisters don't, but
we do. Of course, I don't know how she'll find a buyer for her house. It
needs so much work. The family can help her some, but you know how
that goes."

More than ever, I wanted to do something to help Mrs. Sullivan.
Surely there was more I could do than drive her sister to the grocery
store.

"Yoo-hoo," Leona called, smiling and waving down the block.

I saw three older black ladies coming toward us, all dressed up as
Leona was, smiling and waving back. I recognized them from the
funeral.

"I know this may seem strange, us going out like this so soon after,"
Leona said. "But the Lord's made his decision and taken Arthur. We
need to move on."

I followed Leona down the sidewalk where we met the other ladies,
and introductions were made.

"Dana's going to drive us today," Leona said, then turned to me.
"Leonard used to drive us."

Dora looked closer at me. "You were at the funeral yesterday,
weren't you? With Slade. Lordy, that was one good looking man."

The other women crooned their agreement.

"Is he your boyfriend?" Helen asked.

"No," I said. "We're just friends."

"Good," Helen declared, "because I'm going to fix him up with my
granddaughter."

"Your granddaughter?" Dora asked. She shook her head. "I'd rather keep him for myself."

"Don't even think about it," Ruby told them. "He gave me his cell phone number."

All the ladies laughed.

"Bless your heart for driving today," Dora said to me. "We need to get there. I'm feeling hot."

"Dora's got a system," Ruby explained.

"Dora's got no system," Helen insisted. "She's talking like she's got a system, but all she's got is luck. Plain, ordinary luck."

"Her mojo is working," Helen declared. "I always stand next to her. It rubs off."

"Where, exactly, are we going?" I asked.

"To bingo," Dora said. "Wednesdays. That's our bingo day."

"The four of us, plus Gladys," Ruby said. "And Ida Mayhew, except she isn't coming today."

Dora lowered her voice. "Ida is … taking care of some business."

It flashed in my mind that something had happened to Ida. Hadn't Nick told me that Gerald Mayhew was nowhere to be found? Had he done something to Ida, and disappeared?

"What kind of business?" I asked.

"The kind of business she should have taken care of a long time ago," Ruby declared.

"Is she okay?" I asked.

Ruby waved away my question. "Don't give it a thought. Ida's fine—and she'll be much better soon."

I didn't know what all the cryptic talk was about, but I figured that if something serious were wrong, Ruby would have said so.

"Let's roll," Helen declared.

"You can just drop us off," Leona said to me, "and pick us up after you get off work this evening."

I glanced at my two-door Honda parked at the curb. No way could I fit all these ladies in it, not with those big hats, bigger hips, and large handbags.

"Ladies, I'm sorry, but my car isn't roomy enough for everyone," I said. "There's no way all of you will fit."

"Oh, that's all right," Leona declared. "Gladys said we can use her car. My son, Edward, he got it from her garage last night and brought it over."

I followed the ladies around the corner of the house and stopped dead in my tracks. In front of the Wiley's detached garage sat the Batmobile.

Okay, it was really a Cadillac Coupe de Ville, late 50's model, I guessed. Black, with fins and white wall tires, only slightly shorter than the Queen Mary but just about as wide. A convertible, no less.

"It's Arthur's car," Leona explained, as the ladies climbed inside. "He bought it years ago."

I'd wanted to do something to help, and here was my chance. I slid in behind the wheel.

The interior of the Caddie looked as it must have looked the day it was driven off the showroom floor—gleaming chrome, white supple leather. I cranked up the engine, shifted into gear, and barely touched the gas pedal. The car roared out of the driveway.

"Where's the church?" I asked, as we careened around the corner.

"We're not going to the church," Helen said. "We're going to the Indian casino."

"I'm part Indian," Dora declared. "That's why my mojo works so good there."

I felt like the Grand Marshall of the Rose Parade driving the lead float, as we headed down State Street.

There were a number of Indian casinos throughout Southern California, all of them very popular. The one in Santa Flores had opened several years ago but I'd never been there.

I'd heard about it, though. Not only was there a casino and a bingo hall, but slot machines, restaurants, a buffet, gift shop, and a theater that booked A-list entertainers. A hotel had recently been added.

I headed west on the freeway, then took the Jackson Park exit and turned into the casino entrance. A massive parking structure loomed. I drove in, circled several floors, finally found an empty space, and performed a docking maneuver Captain Picard would have envied.

The ladies piled out of the car, chatting and laughing, and I followed feeling responsible for them, wanting to make sure they were settled before I left them here.

We took the elevator to the casino level and headed toward the *pinging* and *ponging* of the slot machines. The walkway was bright and clean, with large windows opening to the north and south that offered views of the mountains and the whole Santa Flores valley.

A security guard was on duty but he didn't stop us; nobody in this crew looked young enough to be carded.

Inside the casino sat row after row of slot machines with brightly lit screens luring gamblers into risking more money than they would likely get back. The atmosphere reminded me of Las Vegas, but without the glitz and glamour. Here, middle-class housewives, soccer moms, overweight men, and the probably unemployed, sat with glazed stares, feeding the machines.

"There's a card room," Helen said, gesturing through the casino. "I never play cards, but Ruby does."

Ruby gave me a confident not and left. Helen followed.

"I've got to find me a machine. I can feel my mojo working already," Dora announced, then disappeared into the rows of slots.

The ladies seemed to know their way around the place, but I felt a little uncomfortable leaving them here all alone with no transportation. It would be hours before I'd come back.

"Are you sure you'll be okay if I leave?" I asked.

"Sure," Leona said. "Leonard used to leave us. He'd stay sometimes, though, and gamble a little. He liked the slots. He was good at them, but not as good as Dora. Nobody's got mojo like Dora."

The mention of Leonard's name jarred me.

"Do you think he might be here?" I asked, gazing around the casino.

Maybe," Leona said. She looked around, then said. "There's a friend of his. Why don't you ask her?"

I rose on my toes and craned my neck. "Where?"

"Over there at the Lucky Five slot machine," Leona said, pointing. "That white girl with the blond hair."

I followed her finger and my breath caught.

Sitting at the slot machine was Belinda Griffin.

CHAPTER SEVENTEEN

"That woman over there? The blonde in the red blouse?" I asked Leona. "Are you sure?"

"Sure, I'm sure," she replied.

"She's Leonard's friend?" I asked.

"I used to see them talking," Leona said.

This was bizarre. I was here attempting to redeem myself for my failure to locate Leonard Sullivan, only to stumble over a friend of his, Belinda Griffin. The same Belinda Griffin who had a mortgage loan with Mid-America that had been headed for foreclosure when her house burned down.

"Were they involved with each other?" I asked.

"Oh, no, nothing like that," Leona said. "They met here a while back when Leonard was driving us to our weekly bingo game."

"She was here that often?" I asked.

"Just about every time we were here," Leona said. "Well, bye, honey. I've got to catch up with the other girls."

"I'll pick you up after five," I called.

I turned back toward Belinda. She must have sensed something because she looked back at me that same instant. Recognition bloomed on her face. She punched the cash-out button on the machine, grabbed her ticket and took off.

This troubled me. Did she really think that I would approach her here and ask about her past-due payments and possible foreclosure? Did she think I was that callous?

Apparently so.

I wove my way through the rows of slot machines, and watched as Belinda hurried down the wide corridor toward the parking garage.

Then something else hit me. Maybe I wasn't the callous one. It was Belinda, whose house had burned down; Belinda who didn't have a home, a stick of furniture, or a personal belonging—not to mention she had two little children and a husband who might need comforting at this difficult time. And she was here gambling?

I left the casino and cranked up the Caddie. A great deal of work awaited me at the office so I didn't want to take the time to retrieve my Honda from Leona's house, then go back and get the Caddie after work to pick up the ladies, so I drove straight to the office.

I hit the freeway and it occurred to me that maybe I didn't really have to rush back. Manny was probably still in Riverside talking to the district manager, so I saw no reason not to extend my lunch hour. Besides, I was getting the feel of the Caddie. I hit the gas and it accelerated effortlessly up to the speed limit, and then some.

Since picking up Leona and the other ladies I hadn't been able to get Gladys Sullivan off of my mind. Of course, I didn't expect her to join the bingo trip today, so soon after her husband's death. But I wondered if she'd ever be able to go again.

I knew the Sullivans' financial situation had been precarious for a long time. But after what Leona had said today, it troubled me even more. Mrs. Sullivan might have to move out of the house. Her home. The only thing she had left.

Still, selling it would solve many of her problems—the financial ones, anyway. With the money left over from the sale she could pay off all her bills and put the rest away for living expenses, which should be minimal since Leona had offered to share her home.

I mulled this over as the Caddie purred along the freeway. In my position as asset manager for Mid-America, I was strictly prohibited from paying any amount of money on a customer's account. I wasn't, however, restricted from any other form of financial help.

I hadn't been able to stop Mr. Sullivan's murder, identify the man in the house that night, or find Leonard. But I could do something to help, something more than cruise to the Indian casino in the Cadillac.

Since Mrs. Sullivan intended to sell her house—the obvious solution to her financial woes—it seemed to me that I could help in that endeavor. If I could spend an unseemly amount of money on boots for a Halloween costume, I could spend money to have the Sullivans' house painted.

The new coat of paint that Mr. Sullivan had inquired about from Kirk Redmond's contracting business would go a long way toward improving the salability of the home. And if something changed and Mrs. Sullivan decided not to sell, it was still a nice thing for me to do.

A little of the weight I'd been carrying around with me for days now lifted from my shoulders. I'd contact the contractor and make arrangements to have the house painted.

I swung the Caddie into the office parking lot, took up two spaces, and went inside. As I suspected, Manny hadn't returned from his meeting with the district manager which gave Inez the excuse she wanted to glare at me as I passed her desk. I could tell she was winding up for her where-were-you speech so I picked up my phone as soon as I got to my desk.

I called Kirk Redmond's office. Voicemail picked up. I left a message.

I was slightly bummed that my act of kindness was put on hold, so I took care of a few things I was actually being paid to do, then called again. Kirk Redmond answered.

I identified myself and said, "I want to talk to you about Arthur Sullivan. I knew you were at his house."

A long pause followed, and after a while I wondered if we'd been cut off.

"Hello? Mr. Redmond?"

"Yeah," he said. "I'm here."

The man didn't exactly have the best phone manners, but I pressed on.

"There're a couple of things I'd like to clarify," I said, thinking I should get the details of the job—like the price—before I told him to proceed. "Can we do this over the phone, or should I come by your place?"

Another lengthy pause. Finally I heard papers shuffling in the background, Redmond looking up the estimate he'd given Mr. Sullivan, no doubt.

"I'll get back with you," he said.

I wondered how he managed to keep his business going with this crappy attitude. Still, it didn't deter me nor tarnish my good intentions.

"That's fine," I said, and gave him my cell and work numbers. Then it occurred to me that I didn't have the slightest idea what a painting estimate should entail, so I gave him my parents' name and home phone number since I'd need my dad to act as a translator.

We hung up and I drew a breath, altogether pleased with myself for my brilliant idea and my generosity. I dashed off a quick text message to my dad explaining that Redmond would call and that I'd fill him in on the details later.

My personal mojo seemed to be working for me so I pulled out Leonard Sullivan's file folder and once again phoned all of his family and friends hoping that maybe I could at least get a new lead on him.

Everyone pleasantly and willingly gave info, but I learned nothing new. No one knew where to find him.

My personal mojo got worse when Manny walked into the office. He looked even more stressed than usual.

"I need you to go to a house," he said, dropping into his chair.

I managed not to groan aloud. The last thing I wanted was to talk to yet another Mid-America customer who might lose their home. I kept my thoughts to myself, though, since Manny didn't look any happier than I felt at the moment.

"Janet Teague," he said, thrusting a file at me. "Talk to her. Find out what's going on. Get inside. See what kind of shape the house is in. You know the drill."

Yes, unfortunately I did.

"She's probably at work right now," I said.

Manny gave me a just-handle-it wave, and turned away.

When I take over the world, rest assured everybody is going to be able to make their mortgage payment.

At the end of the day, I left the office along with everyone else and slipped behind the wheel of the Caddie. Before I could close the door, Nick walked up.

"Nice ride, Batgirl," he said. "Got a few minutes? There's a café around the corner."

I stepped out of the car. "Why do you try and feed me all the time? Do I look undernourished, or something?"

Nick took several seconds to look me up and down, then said, "You look hot, Dana."

My self-esteem meter jumped off the scale.

Nick nodded toward the corner. "Let's get something to eat and I'll tell you about my day."

"Is this something I want to hear?" I asked.

"Come with me and you'll find out," he told me.

I glanced at my wristwatch. I'd told the ladies I'd pick them up after five, but I figured they wouldn't mind waiting a little longer.

Nick and I walked around the corner to a little restaurant. It had ferns and ceiling fans, and café style tables with green cushions on the chairs. Most of their business came from the lunch crowd, so Nick and I had the place to ourselves this late in the day.

We ordered sandwiches and drinks at the counter. Nick picked up the tab—one of the benefits of looking hot, I suppose.

We sat at a table by the front window sipping our drinks. Outside, traffic was heavy as the office and government buildings emptied out for the night.

"Do I get to hear about your day now?" I asked.

"Not on an empty stomach," Nick said. "Let me hear about your day."

My first thought was to tell him that everything was great, but instead I went with the truth.

"Things could be better, work-wise," I said. "There's a guy who's making me crazy. He's so irritating. You know, if I could pick out one person I could run over with my car, he'd be the one."

Nick nodded. "I know the feeling."

The waitress brought our sandwiches. We ate and talked a little, mostly about nothing. It was nice talking about nothing with Nick.

When we finished, Nick dumped our trash, refilled our drinks and sat down at the table again.

"Today," he said, "was a day of good fortune."

Must have been something big, coming from a homicide detective in the Murder Capital of America.

"I found your jealous husband, the security guard," Nick said.

"Gerald Mayhew?" My excitement spiked. "Did he murder Mr. Sullivan? Did he confess?"

"No. But he did come up with a better alibi," Nick said. "Seems Mayhew wasn't at work the night of the murder because he was at his girlfriend's house."

"What?" I nearly came out of my chair. "He accused his wife of cheating on him with Mr. Sullivan and, all along, he had a girlfriend himself?"

Nick nodded. "That's about the size of it."

"That dog," I said.

"I talked to the girlfriend and another witness who saw them together the night of the murder. Air-tight alibi," Nick said. "Unfortunately, all of this unfolded in front of Mayhew's wife. She didn't take it well."

"Serves the bastard right," I said.

No wonder Ida hadn't gone to bingo today. She'd left her husband.

While I was good with Gerald Mayhew getting what he deserved, it left me without a murder suspect.

Nick seemed to read my mind.

"So Mayhew's out of the picture," he said. "Who else have you got for me, Inspector Gadget?"

"Aren't you supposed to develop some leads yourself?" I asked.

"Didn't we agree on a mutual exchange of information?" he countered.

We had. And I'd been holding back telling him about Leonard Sullivan, thinking it was a family situation and nothing more. Now, though, a weird little knot in my stomach had gotten tighter since this afternoon when Leona Wiley had pointed out Belinda Griffin to me as one of Leonard's friends.

Nick had successfully debunked my Mayhew-as-murderer theory. Maybe he could relieve my anxiety over Leonard. Maybe he could even help me find him.

"Mr. Sullivan's grandson Leonard," I said.

"What about him?"

"He's missing ... sort of," I said.

Nick's detective scowl settled over his face. "How is someone *sort of* missing?"

"No one has seen Leonard since the day of Mr. Sullivan's death," I said. "Gladys Sullivan told me he was at the house that afternoon, and he and Mr. Sullivan had a terrible argument."

"About what?"

"She didn't know. She got scared and left," I said. "But she did say that Mr. Sullivan threatened to go to the police about it."

"You're thinking Leonard might have killed his grandfather?" Nick asked.

"No, I'm not thinking that at all," I said, not sure why I still felt inclined to defend Leonard. "He might have witnessed something and that's why he ran away."

"Or he might have disappeared because he's an accomplice," Nick said.

"Maybe he's hiding because he's scared," I said.

"Maybe he's hiding because he's guilty," Nick said.

Nick and his cop-logic were starting to annoy me.

"Listen," I said, "I just wanted to mention it to you."

He nodded. "I'll check into it. Anything else?"

"No," I said, not feeling the urge to share anything more with him. "What about you?"

"Actually, I do have some information," Nick said. "We turned up something on the contractor who'd been at the Sullivan house."

My stomach did an oh-no lurch.

"Kirk Redmond?" I asked.

"It looks as if he might not be the solid-gold businessman he portrays himself to be," Nick said.

I gulped. "What's going on?"

"I'll let you know when I find out."

I started to tell Nick that I'd phoned Redmond about the painting job at Mr. Sullivan's house, but decided not to. I could always back out of the painting deal if Nick's investigation turned up something.

* * *

When I got to the Indian casino and found the ladies playing slots, they were all in high spirits.

"I told you!" Dora declared. "I told you my mojo was working today!"

"Yeah, it was working, all right," Helen said.

"Worked good for me, too," Ruby said. "I stood right beside her."

"How did you do?" I asked.

"Seven hundred dollars," Dora announced.

My mouth dropped open. Wow, that woman had serious mojo, all right.

"You know what we need?" Ruby said. "We need a trip to Vegas."

"Yeah, let's go to Vegas," Helen agreed.

"Let's do it!" Leona said.

"And Dana can drive us!" Dora said.

The conversation took off from there, totally out of control as the women made plans for the big trip. I never committed to anything but they didn't seem to notice.

I pulled away from Leona's house thinking that I should go by Janet Teague's place, as Manny had instructed, but I just wasn't up to it tonight.

I glanced in the rearview mirror at the ladies standing on the front lawn still talking about the Vegas trip that I'd somehow gotten involved in.

I hoped this was my only act of generosity that blew up in my face.

CHAPTER EIGHTEEN

Thursday morning I awoke without the jubilant feeling that particular day of the week usually brought. I got out of bed and Seven Eleven went down the hallway with me, both of us stretching and yawning.

She came fully awake at the sound of the canned cat food being opened, and I came awake at the smell. I put it in her dish, freshened her water, and poured myself some orange juice.

All sorts of thoughts had run through my head since I'd had dinner with Nick last night. A lot of them were about Nick, of course, but most involved the other things that had gone on yesterday.

Such as spotting Belinda Griffin in the Indian casino. What was that all about? Maybe she'd just needed a break, as Leona Wiley and the other ladies had who'd endured a family crisis. But the look on Belinda's face when she'd seen me gave me an odd feeling.

And, of course, my upcoming trip to Vegas was in my thoughts. In my zeal to help out Mrs. Sullivan's family I'd somehow gotten hooked into a trip to Sin City with the ladies in the Caddie. I'm still not sure exactly how my act of kindness had gone so wrong.

Also, Kirk Redmond hadn't called me back yet about painting Mr. Sullivan's house, and I'd expected that he would. Even if he'd called my dad, I'd have heard about it. But after what Nick had said about Redmond being a questionable businessman—and possibly a murder suspect—maybe it was for the best.

Another of my great intentions shot down.

I wondered if I should tell Nick about my attempt to contact Redmond, but didn't see what good it would do. Failure to return a phone call wasn't a crime, though when I took over the world I'd strongly consider enacting just such a law.

As I got dressed for work, I decided that my day needed a lift. The new thigh-high boots I'd bought for my pirate costume came to mind. I went into my second bedroom and eyed the box. The temptation to wear them to work today nearly overcame me. The look on Inez's face when she saw me walk into the office in those things would carry me through the day easily.

I resisted with some effort and turned to leave when the yellow legal tablet beside the computer caught my eye.

I'd used the circles on the pad to try and figure out how everyone was connected to Mr. Sullivan, sort of like a connect-the-dots game. So far, I'd come up with nothing but theories that hadn't panned out. My "dots" hadn't taken me very far.

I turned the tablet sideways. Maybe I needed to look at the murder from a different angle. Maybe Mr. Sullivan wasn't the central figure, even though he was the victim.

Turning to a fresh page, I drew a big circle and put Leonard's name in it. Was he the center of this whole thing?

I made more circles, connecting Leonard to Mr. Sullivan. In that circle I noted Leonard's argument—the possible motive—and his disappearance. Belinda Griffin connected with Leonard, thanks to their chats at the casino.

And what about the guy who'd accosted me at the post office and at Club Vibe? Nothing connected him to Leonard, yet I couldn't help but write in a question mark to represent him. I did the same with Jarrod Parker because he'd acted so weird lately, and left those two circles floating, not connected to anything.

I stared at the legal pad. The new configuration of circles didn't spark my imagination.

Then just for the heck of it, I started a new page, this time putting Kirk Redmond's name in the center circle. Aside from his connection to the Sullivan home and Nick's vague comment, I was unable to draw more circles. Another dead end.

Annoyed with the whole thing—and myself—I dropped the legal pad beside the computer, finished getting dressed, and left. As I headed for work I cranked up the CD trying to chase away a little nagging thought that had taken root in my mind.

Mr. Sullivan's murder, Leonard's disappearance, Belinda's house burning down. A lot of bad things had been falling down around me. How long before something bad landed on me?

* * *

One nice thing about having a job was that if the rest of your life was a mess, being at work was a good place to get your mind off your problems. That's because there's a whole other set of problems waiting for you there.

The routine of the office felt comfortable when I walked in. For better or worse, these were the people I spent most of my time with. I took a deep breath, settled into my desk, and decided that no matter what, today I would have a good day.

My resolve was tested almost immediate after Manny arrived. He called me to his desk.

"What's up on the Parker repo?" he asked, gesturing to his computer screen. "I told the DM the account would be cleared by the end of the week. That's tomorrow."

"It will be," I assured him.

Really, I didn't know that for sure. But I had a strong feeling that Jarrod could get the money to pay off the account and pick up his car, and I couldn't imagine him facing the weekend without his hot Mustang convertible to drive around in.

"What about Janet Teague?" Manny asked, flipping to another screen. "Did you make contact? Find out what she intends to do about her house?"

Manny had given me this account to work and I hadn't done much of anything about it, which was bad, of course. This was no way to keep my job, so I was forced to tell a lie.

"I went by her place last night and sat there for over an hour. She never showed," I said. "I'll go out again today."

Manny clicked the mouse to pull up another account on his computer. I figured this was the perfect time to distract him.

"I saw Belinda Griffin yesterday playing slots at the Indian casino," I said.

Manny just shook his head. He'd been in this business a long time, much longer than me. After a while, I guess nothing was surprising.

"That whole deal is weird," I said. "Their beautiful home, all the work they'd put into the backyard. Then Belinda acts like it's nothing when it burns down."

Manny just shrugged.

"I understand the fire is being investigated as arson," I said.

"Great," he grumbled.

I went back to my desk and got to work. I barely noticed when Manny left the office. Carmen brought me a sandwich when she came back from lunch.

"Dana," Inez said, taking off her glasses as she walked to my desk.

"Did Manny authorize your in-place, overtimelunch before he left?"

"Yes," I lied.

Inez folded her arms. "Now, Dana, I showed you Corporate's memo on overtime. Do I need to staple it to your desk?"

I was ready to staple it to Inez's forehead when Carmen interrupted.

"Sean Griffin is here," she said in a low voice. News that the Griffins' house had burned down had already made the rounds in the office.

"Manny should talk to Mr. Griffin," Inez said. "But since he's not here, I'll handle it myself."

"I've got it," I said, and pushed past her.

Carmen gave me the Griffin account summary she'd printed and I went into the interview room where Sean Griffin waited. I introduced myself and sat down across the table from him.

I'd never seen him before. His file indicated he was in his early thirties, and he looked it. Attractive, but not handsome. Dark hair, medium height. He had on a faded T-shirt, denim jeans and jacket.

Sean didn't seem to match Belinda. She looked sleek and fashionable. Sean looked as if he worked hard for a living at his factory job.

He looked uncomfortable in the office. Uncomfortable in his skin. Maybe even uncomfortable in his life—most of which was attributable to the fact that his house and everything he owned had gone up in flames a few days ago.

I wasn't sure why he was here so I kept my mouth shut and waited him out. It took him a few minutes to get started because I don't think he knew why he was here, either. Finally, he pulled a handful of envelopes out of his jacket pocket.

"The post office has been holding our mail since the house ... went," Sean said. "I picked these up this morning."

He placed the envelopes on the table. I saw return addresses from several credit card and utility companies.

"I've never heard of some of these places. The balances are in the thousands, and the payments are all past due." Sean dragged his palm over his forehead. "I don't understand."

I didn't need to look inside the envelopes to know Sean was right. I'd seen the past due balances on their credit report when I'd gone out to their house.

He gazed across the table at me. "How can this be possible?"

Lucky me, I had to deliver yet another piece of unwelcome news to a man already drowning in it.

"Your account with us is behind, too," I said. "Four months behind."

Sean rocked back in his chair. "I didn't want to take out a second mortgage on the house. I didn't want all that work done in the backyard. I told Belinda it wasn't a good idea, but she insisted."

"Sorry, but we've started foreclosure proceedings," I said, feeling like a complete jerk.

Sean squeezed his eyes shut for a few seconds, then shook his head.

"But why did this happen? How did it happen? I make plenty of money. I give my paycheck to Belinda every week to take care of this stuff. Why is this happening?"

I was getting a sick feeling in my stomach because I thought I knew the answers to Sean's questions.

I thought Sean knew, too.

"Belinda wasn't paying the bills, was she?" I asked quietly.

I guess hearing it spoken aloud was too much for Sean. He cursed softly and slumped down in his chair.

"She was supposed to take care of all this," he said. "I went to the bank before I came here. We had a good chunk of savings—but not anymore. It's gone. Why would she do this? Where did all the money go?"

"Have you talked with her about it?" I asked.

Sean shook his head. "I don't know where she is."

"Aren't you staying with friends?" I asked. "That's what Belinda told us when she called my boss about the fire."

His gaze came up sharply. "She's with a friend? Here in town?"

An icky knot jerked in my stomach. I couldn't think of anything to say but Sean didn't give me a chance anyway.

"We had a fight last week," he said. "She told me to leave. I've been staying with a buddy of mine from work. And now she's staying with her *friend*?"

From the look on Sean's face, I knew he suspected—or knew—that Belinda's friend was really a boyfriend.

He gathered the envelopes from the desk and stuffed them into his pocket again.

"I'm really sorry about all these problems," I said, though my words seemed woefully lacking. What do you say to a man who's lost everything he has in the world?

"The foreclosure will be on hold until the insurance claim is settled," I said, hoping it would be at least a tiny piece of good news.

"I'm getting my daughters back," he said, with a determination that surprised me. "She's not taking my girls, on top of everything else."

Sean left the office. I sat there for a while feeling bad for him, thinking how my own problems seemed small.

Sean had put his time, money, and emotions into building a life. He had a good job, a nice home, a wife and two little girls.

But that was last week. This week, everything was different.

I wondered how Belinda, who supposedly loved Sean, could have done such a selfish thing. She'd taken his hard-earned money that was meant for their family and spent it on something else. She'd ruined their credit. She'd let their home go to foreclosure. She'd kicked Sean out and left with his kids. And all along, she'd had a boyfriend.

A little chill swept over me. If Belinda was capable of all that, what else might she do?

CHAPTER NINETEEN

Friday. My favorite day of the week.

Usually.

The problem with this particular Friday was that it wouldn't mark the end of my week. Corporate insisted the Mid-America offices remain open one Saturday out of the month, and tomorrow was it. Though working would cut into my time to prepare for Felderman's Halloween party on Saturday night, I was still glad I had a job.

I settled into my desk vowing to have a good day. Fridays should always be good days.

That's one of the things I'm definitely doing when I take over the world.

Things went well for a few hours until Carmen appeared in front of my desk wearing a frown.

Not a good sign.

"Jarrod Parker is here," she said.

I'd been on the telephone and hadn't seen him come into the office.

This could go either way, I decided, as I pulled up his account on my computer and printed the summary. Either he'd pay what he owed, or he'd ruin my day.

Somehow, I already knew the answer.

Jarrod proved to be full of surprises, though, when I sat down across the table from him in the interview room and he pulled out a wad of bills.

"I'm paying off my account," he said, and smiled as if this would impress me. "Does that make you happy, Dana?"

"Hang on a minute," I said.

I went to the front counter and asked Carmen to come into the office with me. Not that I needed backup. Carmen was responsible for all the monetary transactions in our office so she had to be present whenever any money—especially a large amount of cash—was involved.

Jarrod counted out the money required to payoff his account—a little over seven grand, which he had down to the penny—then Carmen re-counted it with him watching. I counted along, too. I didn't want him coming back later claiming we'd short-changed him, or something.

Carmen, cash in hand, and I went back to the front counter where she posted the money to Jarrod's account leaving a zero-balance, and printed a receipt.

Mid-America had a limit on the amount of cash allowed in the office at any given time. In case of a robbery—not a farfetched scenario in the Murder Capital of America—Corporate wanted the bad guys to get away with the least amount of money possible. I couldn't disagree with their thinking. Mid-America was self-insured. If we suffered a loss, we ate it.

This chunk of cash that Jarrod had presented us with put the office way over our exposure limit. Carmen gave me Jarrod's receipt and started balancing her cash drawer. She'd be off to the bank to make the deposit within minutes.

I pulled his file from the cabinet and completed the paperwork to close out his account and release the lien on his Mustang. I called Quality Recovery and told the receptionist the auto had been redeemed and we were returning it to the customer. She promised to get it to our office pronto.

They were good about delivering a vehicle to our office right away. They understood that the relationship with our customer had completely broken down at that point, and it was awkward to have them sitting around our office for a long time.

I went back into the interview room and presented Jarrod with his paperwork.

"Your car will be delivered in a few minutes," I told him. "You can go grab a coffee at the café around the corner."

"I'll wait here," he said.

Just my luck.

Jarrod could wait if he wanted to, but I was under no obligation to entertain him while he did. I left him alone in the interview room.

Inez loomed over the front counter when I walked out. Carmen was having trouble balancing her cash drawer, probably because of a posting error she'd made earlier in the day. It required her to go through each transaction to locate her mistake, then correct it. It was time-consuming and tedious work. Inez was asking her questions—her version of helping—which only distracted Carmen and prolonged the process.

I went back to my desk and accessed Jarrod's account on my

computer, and took a minute to savor the zero in the balance column. He was a first-class jerk, but he wasn't my problem anymore.

I walked over to Manny's desk and gave him the news.

"Good job, Dana, good job," he said. "I'll let the DM know. He'll be glad that account is off our books, and we're not saddled with an auto we'll have to sell."

When I turned back to my desk I noticed Jade standing in the doorway of the interview room. Her hair whipped around as if she were standing in a wind tunnel, so I knew she was talking to Jarrod.

For a second or two, I wondered who Jarrod's current girlfriend might be, then was saved from the nauseating mental picture by Slade. He stepped into the office, waved, then went outside again. I grabbed Jarrod's file, a clipboard and a vehicle inspection report, and headed for the door.

"Your car's here," I called to Jarrod over Jade's shoulder.

He bolted past her and followed me into the parking lot.

Slade had driven the Mustang to our office and parked it at the rear of the lot away from the other cars. He stood at the rear bumper looking hot in jeans and a snug T-shirt.

I went over the car checking off the boxes on the vehicle inspection form, then compared it to the report I'd completed the morning Slade and I had repo'd it. The vehicle was in identical shape. No dents or dings incurred while in the possession of Quality Recovery.

I made Jarrod go over the Mustang, too. In the past, a few customers had claimed their vehicle had been damaged while in our possession. It always got messy.

Jarrod looked over his car, started the engine, cranked up the radio, and finally declared it was in good condition. I made him sign a form to that effect, and Slade had him sign something similar for Quality Recovery.

"That's it?" Jarrod asked.

"That's it," I told him, and pressed my lips together to keep from adding "and good riddance."

Jarrod hesitated before getting into the Mustang.

"So, Dana, when will I see you again?" he asked.

"Never," I told him.

"Well, what about if I need another loan?" Jarrod asked. "I mean, I did pay off the account."

"Forget it," I said.

He slid into the Mustang and ran down the window.

"See you around, Dana," he called.

"No, you won't!" I shouted.

But it was no good. Jarrod smiled and waved as he drove out of the parking lot.

I stood there watching him, thankful he was gone but visualizing my hands closing around his neck. Slade walked up, shattering my perfectly good daydream.

He put his hand on my shoulder. "It's cool, babe."

I blew out a heavy breath. "Yeah, I guess."

We walked toward the office building.

"Everything okay with you?" Slade asked.

He surprised me with his insight and concern. We'd had our share of moments together in the last week or so, as I'd never expected.

"Yeah, kind of," I said.

"Tell your folks to stay away from that contractor," Slade said.

I stopped short. I'd forgotten that I'd asked Slade about Kirk Redmond by pretending I wanted the information for my parents.

"Why?" I asked. "What's wrong with him?"

"He's not much of a contractor," he said.

Nick flashed in my mind and his comment about Kirk Redmond being less than a solid-gold businessman.

"He's more like a drug dealer," Slade said.

"What?"

Slade looked down at me. "The business is a cover. He works just enough to make it look legit. Way I hear it, he's got a network of dealers working for him like you wouldn't believe. The man's well connected."

"What?"

"Tell your folks to steer clear of him," Slade said. "He's bad news."

Stunned, I walked with Slade across the parking lot. Kirk Redmond was a drug dealer? And I'd called and talked to him about Mr. Sullivan. No way was I getting involved with him. When Redmond called back about the paint estimate, I'd tell him to forget the whole thing.

"Later," Slade called as he headed off down Fifth Street.

"Thanks," I called.

He waved and kept walking.

I headed for the office door when I saw a blue Chevy pickup swing into the parking lot. I recognized Sean Griffin behind the wheel. I waited on the sidewalk for him while he parked. A little breeze blew, stirred up by the cars going past. Sean got out of his truck and walked over. He had on the same shirt I'd seen him in yesterday. He looked tired.

He stopped beside me. "I saw Belinda last night."

"How'd it go?" I asked.

"I told her I was coming today to pick up the girls," Sean said.

The sidewalk in front of the office was no place for this conversation. "Let's go inside," I said.

The office door opened and Carmen walked out with the deposit bag tucked under her arm, on her way to the bank to deposit Jarrod's cash. She smiled and walked past us. Sean reached behind me to hold the door open.

A car on Fifth Street slowed down at the curb. The window rolled down. The man in the passenger seat pointed a gun at me. Two shots rang out.

Carmen screamed. Sean pushed me, knocking me to the sidewalk. Tires squealed and the engine roared.

My heart pounded. I lay on the sidewalk for a couple of seconds, stunned, not sure exactly what had happened. My mind wouldn't process the information.

Carmen's screams penetrated my confusion. I rolled cover and sat up. She stood about ten feet away, hands against her cheeks, still screaming.

Beside me, Sean Griffin was slumped against the building, his legs stretched out in front of him, two blood-soaked holes in his chest.

I surged to my feet. A wave of horror washed over me. I stared at Sean. He'd pushed me down. Pushed me to safety.

Slade appeared out of nowhere. He grabbed Carmen by the arm and pulled her toward the office door. He pushed me in ahead of her.

"Call 9-1-1," he said. "Stay inside."

Manny was already at the front of the office when we got inside, Inez on his heels. He snatched up the telephone on the front counter and punched in the numbers. I pushed Carmen toward Inez and ran back outside.

Slade laid Sean flat on the sidewalk and knelt over him. I dropped to his side.

Blood pumped out of Sean's chest saturating his shirt, his arms, pooling around him. Slade bent and listened at his mouth.

"Is he breathing?" I asked, hearing the desperation in my voice.

"He's breathing, but he's going to bleed out before the medics get here." Slade pulled off his T-shirt, doubled it over and pressed it against Sean's chest.

I'd never felt so helpless, so useless, so worthless in my life.

But I couldn't just sit there. I scooted around to Sean's head and stroked his hair. His eyes opened, but I saw no recognition in them only a dull, glassy look. They fell shut again. Color drained from his face.

What I did served no medical purpose, only offered some measure of comfort in what I feared were Sean Griffin's last minutes on this earth.

Slade looked at me as if he read my thoughts. He shook his head. Tears burned my eyes.

The wail of a sirén drew closer and an ambulance drove into our parking lot. Paramedics pulled Slade and me away and went to work on Sean. A crowd gathered on the sidewalk. Two police cars screeched to a stop at the curb. Several uniforms piled out.

I stood there staring at Sean. The paramedics put tubes in him, forced a bag over his mouth, injected him with something.

But I knew it was too late.

I'd seen Mr. Sullivan.

The uniforms pushed the crowd back and another vehicle pulled into the parking lot. Nick got out.

I ran to him. Uninvited, shamelessly, I threw my arms around him and he pulled me against him.

"What happened, Dana?" he asked against my cheek.

"Sean Griffin was shot," I whispered, barely able to get the words out. "He was shot ... instead of me."

CHAPTER TWENTY

Nick took me into the office and left me there. He went back outside. Manny and Lucas watched through the window. Inez and Jade stayed with Carmen in the breakroom, talking softly and holding a cool cloth on her forehead. I heard her sniffling.

I wanted to leave. I wanted to be anywhere but here. I couldn't bear to look out the window. I'd be no help calming Carmen. I just wanted to get away from this place.

But where would I go? Home? No, I didn't want to be alone. My folks' house? I didn't want to tell them what had happened. Not now, anyway.

My adrenaline was pumping, but my legs were wobbly. My hands felt like ice. I collapsed into my desk chair and covered my face with my palms, blocking out the world but finding no respite from my thoughts. Sean Griffin's face floated through my mind.

The usual office sounds went on around me. The telephone rang. Inez took messages. Normal things happened. Just as if Sean Griffin hadn't been gunned down a few feet away because he'd pushed me aside and taken the bullets meant for me.

There really was no justice in the world. Sean, who could have used a little luck in his life, had gotten another bad deal—the final bad deal. It wasn't fair. It just wasn't fair. Sean had gotten shot while that idiot Jarrod Parker had left the scene just moments before.

I didn't wish Jarrod dead—not really. But it just wasn't right that Sean, the good guy, had taken two bullets while Jarrod, the not-so-good-guy, had driven away unscathed. Jarrod didn't even know what had happened. He was tooling the road in his Mustang at this very moment, oblivious to the whole thing.

Jarrod seemed to be one of those people destined to live his entire life in oblivion. He'd been at Club Vibe the Saturday night when I'd gotten jumped in the parking lot and he hadn't known anything about it. Now, here he was a week later and the same thing happened.

Did that guy have incredible luck, or what?

A little jolt in my stomach caused me to sit up straight in my chair. Was something more than good fortune at work here?

I'd considered that there was something odd in Jarrod's change in behavior toward me. Just how odd was it?

Nick came into the office and spoke with Carmen in the breakroom. He talked to everybody else, then came to my desk.

"Come on," he said.

I knew where he was taking me. I got my purse and left the office with him. But I didn't want to sit in a police car, so I pulled myself together enough to take my Honda.

At the police station Nick took me to the same little interview room I'd been in before. He brought coffee and sat down across the table from me.

"Is Sean ... is he—" I couldn't finish the thought.

Nick shook his head. "He didn't make it."

Really I knew that, but a little part of me had held out hope that he'd pulled through, somehow.

"Did you see the gunman?" Nick asked.

"All I saw was the gun." I sipped my coffee. "Could this have been an attempted robbery?"

"Why do you think that?" he asked.

"Carmen had over seven grand in the bank bag," I said. "A customer, Jarrod Parker, had just paid off his account in cash to redeem his car I'd repo'd."

Nick pulled a small tablet from his shirt pocket and wrote down Jarrod's name.

"And you think he might have arranged to have his money returned to him?" he asked.

"I don't know. Maybe." I pushed away my coffee cup. "I guess I just want to blame someone other than myself."

Nick frowned. "Do you think those bullets were meant for you?"

Guilt pressed against my chest making it hard to breath. "Yes," I whispered.

"Griffin was the target," Nick said. "Two witnesses on the street saw the shooting."

The knot in my chest unwound a bit. "Are you sure?" I asked.

"Positive," Nick said. "Why do you think you were the intended victim?"

"It seemed logical," I said. "I mean, why would anybody want Sean Griffin dead? It had to be me."

"Why?" Nick asked again.

I drew in a breath. "Because of my involvement with Mr. Sullivan's murder."

"What involvement?" Nick glared at me. "I told you to stay out of this, Dana."

I heard the anger in his voice, and I got mad, too. I wasn't sure if I was really mad at Nick, or mad at life and taking it out on Nick.

"What about our mutual exchange of information? Have you forgotten about that?" I slammed my fist on the table and pushed to my feet. "And thanks a whole hell of a lot for your concern that I was nearly killed today!"

I snatched up my purse and broke for the door. Nick was faster. He got there first and blocked it with his body.

We glared at each other. Inside, I was boiling. Nick was too. I could see it in his heavy breathing and feel it in the heat he gave off.

This wasn't a battle of wills over a police investigation. It was something more, something deeper. Something personal between Nick and me.

He blinked first. "Dana—"

I darted around him. He didn't come after me.

I bolted for my car and drove away. I wasn't going back to work. It was the middle of the afternoon and I had tons of things to do, but I wasn't going back inside that office. I didn't want to see Sean Griffin's blood stain on the sidewalk. I didn't want to talk to anyone about what had happened.

I swung onto State Street. I didn't know where I wanted to go, really, or who I wanted to be with.

Two blocks later, I admitted to myself that I was lying. I knew who I wanted to be with.

I drove to my apartment, changed into sweats and chugged a beer hoping it would make me sleepy. It didn't.

I hoped it would dissipate the guilty relief I felt over Sean's death not being my fault. It didn't.

I wanted it to make me forget about Nick Travis. That didn't happen, either.

In my second bedroom I got the yellow legal pad and a pencil and took them into the kitchen. I ripped off all the pages I'd written on and spread them out on the table.

So far I'd put just about everyone I knew in the center circle, designating each of them a central character in Mr. Sullivan's murder. Around them, I'd written the names of other people involved, possible clues, and question marks.

It had gotten me nowhere.

I tried them all again. I went through page after page, writing in names, drawing circles, making notes.

Still nothing.

The dots I was trying to connect only went so far. The chain didn't make a complete picture. It didn't lead anywhere, certainly not to a murderer.

Desperate, I tried putting Sean Griffin's name in the center circle, hoping something might present itself. Nothing did.

I sat back in the chair staring at the pages of circles and names, and wondered if I should just accept the fact that none of these people were connected. Maybe it was Leonard all along who'd murdered his grandfather, and I just didn't want to face it. Maybe it was someone I didn't even know about.

The beer finally kicked in. I went to bed even though it wasn't dark yet, and fell asleep.

* * *

I awoke around eleven with a headache caused by all the dreams I'd had, rather than the one beer I'd chugged, and went to the kitchen. I'd left the light on and the room seemed harsh and chilly. I ran a glass of water and downed some aspirin.

I checked my phone and saw that Mom had left me a message. I must have slept hard because I hadn't heard it ring. She asked if I wanted to come over for dinner. Too late for that now.

There was another message, this one from Manny asking if I was all right.

No message from Nick.

I was about to flip off the light and head back to bed when the yellow legal pad on the table caught my eye. Scattered around it were the sheets of paper with all the circles I'd drawn, my supposed suspects, the solid clues, and the unconnected ones I'd thought important.

None of it fit. Even looking at it again, something was missing.

I picked up the pencil and, just for the heck of it, I drew a circle in the center of another sheet of paper. But whose name would I write inside? Who was the central character, the one person connected to everyone and everything?

From somewhere in the back of my mind an idea came to me, an idea born from something I'd heard today. Something Slade had said and I'd forgotten in the midst of all the confusion and emotion.

I wrote down a name—Kirk Redmond. I drew intersecting circles containing clues and suspects. The page filled up fast. All the dots connected.

My headache got worse.

I switched off the light and went back to bed.

* * *

On Saturday morning I put on my running shoes and did a few laps around the parking lot of my apartment complex. Another great Southern California day had dawned, sunshine, warm breeze, and clear skies.

As I jogged along firming my thighs, I realized that in my distress yesterday I hadn't done my usual Friday week-in-review on the drive home.

It had been a mixed week, to say the least. On the plus side, Mom wasn't planning to move out, my parents were speaking again, and they were going to a party together this weekend. Also, Jarrod Parker had paid off his account and was out of my life.

That was about it for good news. Not much to show for a whole week.

On the minus side, for the second week in a row somebody I knew had been murdered. I was two for two.

And my last little bit of bad news for the week was that I'd decided to end my relationship with Nick—if what we had could be called that.

Somehow, even after everything else that had happened, that part of my week-in-review made me the saddest of all.

When I got back to my apartment, I got dressed for work in jeans and a sweater. Saturdays were dress-down days at Mid-America for everyone except Inez, who wore her customary, self-imposed uniform.

I gave Seven Eleven some dry food and a cuddle on my way out the door, then noticed the yellow legal pages I'd left on the table. I looked at them in the cold light of the morning wondering if maybe my headache and the beer I'd drunk last night had made me see things that weren't really there. Now, clear-headed and looking at them again, they still made sense.

If I hadn't been so troubled about Nick I would have phoned him and passed along what I'd come up with. But something was between us.

Really, a lot of things were between us.

I guess it all boiled down to Katie Jo and Nick in high school. I'd crushed on Nick big-time back then. Katie Jo had been my best friend at a time when having a best friend meant everything.

They'd both let me down. On some level I was still mad at them both.

And really, mad at myself too.

When I got to the office, Manny and Inez were there. I didn't know why Inez came in on Saturdays. We didn't need her and we certainly didn't want her.

"How're you holding up?" Manny asked, when I sat down at my desk.

"I'm good," I told him, though I didn't feel that way.

I guess Manny saw through my comment because he said, "You don't have to be here today, if it's too much for you."

I gave him a little smile—the first one I'd felt in a while—and shook my head.

"Thanks, but I'm good," I said.

He nodded toward the front of the room. "Carmen's not coming in today. Her husband called, said she was too upset."

I might have stayed home too if I'd had a husband to call in for me, to cluck over me, to hold my hand and support me. But all I had was an empty apartment, or my folks' place, and neither was as fulfilling as a husband. I found myself a little envious of Carmen.

"I'd rather stay busy," I said. "I've got to make some calls and I've still got to catch up with Janet Teague to look at her house."

Manny nodded and turned back to his work.

I went through my phone route making routine calls. Even though I had to put forth effort to keep my job, my heart wasn't in it.

At noon I told Manny I was going out to try and find Janet Teague, and see what was up with her mortgage payments.

I hit Burger King. There was a newspaper rack in the drive-thru line so I bought a copy and looked through it while I waited for my order.

I steered with my knee and ate as I drove to Leonard's cousin's house in Atwater. I didn't see the Lexus that Leonard was rumored to drive parked at the house or in the neighborhood, so I figured he wasn't there. I drove over to Devon, past the Sullivan house, past Leona's place. No sign of Leonard.

Unless Leonard fell out of the sky on top of me and my little Honda, I didn't expect to see him today—or ever.

All I could think was that I'd failed again.

CHAPTER TWENTY ONE

I'd told Manny I would pay a call on Janet Teague to let her know Mid-America was considering foreclosing on her home. I swung into a strip mall and parked, then flipped through the file I'd brought with me.

Manny worked the mortgage accounts, but I knew Janet Teague well. She was the hot dog lady.

Sometimes when things get busy in the office, I help out taking credit applications from perspective customers. That's how I'd come to meet Janet Teague. In the office that day several months ago, she'd asked for an additional six grand to pay off some bills and to fulfill her life's dream. She wanted to buy a hot dog cart.

Hot dog cart ownership wasn't my idea of a dream come true, but who was I to judge?

The cart she wanted was the kind that could be towed behind a car to swap meets and grand openings. It had an umbrella, steam trays, condiment compartments, an ice bin for cold drinks—all the bells and whistles.

With that cart, Janet declared she would at long last have financial independence. She worked at a warehouse at slightly more than minimum wage, and would probably never do any better.

Janet begged for that loan. She wanted that hot dog cart like I'd never seen anybody want anything. Mid-America had approved the loan, adding the six thousand dollars onto her existing second mortgage account, and after a few months Janet stopped paying. So much for dreams, I guess.

Manny had made numerous attempts to contact Janet, to find out what was going on, see if we could work out some sort of payment arrangement with her. Nothing. Janet hadn't returned one single call.

I was annoyed with her. Begging for the loan, then ignoring the payments. It didn't sit well with me. Lots of people were struggling with financial problems, but they didn't bury their head in the sand and refuse to acknowledge the situation.

Ninth Street wasn't far away so I drove to her house hoping I'd catch her at home. The neighborhood of stucco houses was quiet. I knocked on her door. No answer. I circled to the detached garage at the rear of the lot and peered through the dusty glass windows in the rollup doors. Nothing inside but boxes of Christmas decorations and general junk.

Just as I figured, Janet wasn't at home this lovely Saturday morning. But I had a pretty good idea where to find her.

I went back to my Honda, finished off my soda as I looked through the newspaper again, and headed out Clayton Boulevard to the anniversary celebration at the White Cottage Furniture store I'd seen splashed over the last page of the Living section. According to their advertisement, there would be door prizes, balloons for the kids, food, drinks, and rock bottom prices. I could always use a rock-bottom price on something, but I wasn't in the market for furniture today. I was looking for hot dogs.

As I pulled into the parking lot I saw that the furniture showroom windows were splashed with prices. A row of recliners was sitting on the sidewalk and balloons waved in the breeze. Their food, however, consisted of a popcorn machine. Not what I was looking for.

I continued down Clayton Boulevard to The Work Out Place, a new fitness center that was opening, according to their ad in the newspaper. Several hot looking guys in tight workout clothes offered visitors one day passes, along with trail mix and bottled water. No hot dogs for this crowd.

I caught the freeway and drove to Home Depot, the store I'd been in with Slade last Sunday. They were having their grand re-opening today.

A big banner stretched across the front of the store. The entrance was cluttered with cement blocks, stacks of lumber, and trays of mum plants. A clown was doing face painting for kids, a clerk in a bright red apron handed out balloons, and—sure enough—Janet Teague was manning her hot dog cart.

I thumped my fist against the steering wheel. I might not have found Leonard Sullivan, but Janet was mine.

The parking lot was jammed. I finally found a spot in front of Ryan's Electronics Warehouse that shared the lot with Home Depot, grabbed my handbag and joined the flow of customers headed for homeowner heaven.

I stopped behind a storage shed on display at the front of the building and took a look at Janet. She was working hard. A long line had formed at her cart and she was dishing out dogs, chips, and drinks at record speed.

According to the newspaper advertisement, the grand re-opening celebration was scheduled to last until 4:00 today. I glanced at my watch and saw that it was a little after two o'clock.

No sense in disturbing Janet or discouraging her customers, I decided. She wasn't going anywhere for a while.

I went into Home Depot, wandered around, got bored and left again. Unless you had a home, none of this stuff was even mildly interesting.

I checked on Janet, made sure she was still selling dogs, then ambled next door to Ryan's Electronics Warehouse. Now here was a place to while away the hours.

Windows stretched across the front of the store, so every few minutes I peeked out. Janet hadn't moved. The line of hungry people kept coming.

I looked around, bought two CDs—both 70s mixes my dad would like for Christmas—and took them to my car, then walked to Home Depot again. A set of bleachers outside their entrance had filled up with about a dozen men as the scheduled demonstration was about to begin. I sat down and watched a guy in a Home Depot apron explain the intricacies of grouting a bathtub.

From my seat I could see Janet. Customers still bought food and drinks, but business was waning. Janet looked tired. I was hungry, but I wasn't about to leave, and I certainly wasn't going to buy a hot dog from Janet.

When the tub grouting group broke up, another guy came out and set up for the next demonstration. Gradually, a half dozen or so men joined me on the bleachers, and we turned our attention to learning the craft of tile setting.

I must have gotten pretty caught up in it because I didn't notice Nick until he was standing beside the bleachers at my elbow. He had on jeans and a blue Henley shirt. He looked good. I was surprised to see him.

I guess Nick was more surprised.

"What are you doing here?" he asked.

"I'm thinking of taking on a part-time job," I said, and nodded toward the tile guy. "You?"

"Leaky faucet," he said.

I remembered then that I'd read on Nick's credit application that he owned a home. He really was here for some home improvements. I remembered, too, that I'd decided to end my relationship with him.

This would be the perfect time to tell him, of course, but somehow I couldn't get the words to form. My mind didn't want to create them. My mouth didn't want to speak them. My heart didn't want any part of the whole deal, either.

Nick didn't say anything for a while. He leaned his elbow on the bleachers, almost—but not quite—touching my thigh. We watched the tile setting demonstration for a few minutes.

"I checked on your friend Jarrod Parker," Nick said.

After all that had happened, I'd forgotten I'd mentioned Jarrod to Nick as a possible suspect.

"He's got no record. No ties to anything criminal," Nick said. "I talked to him. He's got an alibi for the Sullivan murder. Nothing connects him to Griffin's death."

I glanced at Janet Teague and her hot dog cart. She hadn't had a customer in a while. I check my watch and saw that it was almost four.

"Look, Nick, I've got something to take care of," I said. "I'll be right back."

I climbed down from the bleachers and walked up to Janet's cart. She was in her early forties, with brown hair pulled back in a scarf and makeup she'd put on badly.

"What'll you have?" she asked, reaching for a bun.

"Hi, Janet."

She looked at me. I saw recognition flash in her eyes.

"Oh …."

"What's going on, Janet?" I asked. "Why haven't you returned any of Manny's phone calls?"

She shrugged. "I didn't know what to tell him."

I leaned in. "You're way behind on your mortgage, Janet. You're about to lose your house. What's going on?"

"I fell and sprained my ankle," Janet said. "I lost my job because I couldn't work, and I had medical bills. Then my car quit running. It's been one awful thing after another for weeks now."

I'd heard similar stories from other customers, good people who got caught in a downward spiral. My heart went out to Janet.

"Your ankle must be better," I said, "if you're working here."

"Oh, yeah, sure it is," she told me, then stuck out here foot and gave it a little shake. "I've got a new job lined up that I'm starting in a week, and I'm getting caught up on things best I can."

"Have you got the money to bring your account up to date?" I asked, really hoping that she'd say she did.

"Half of it," Janet said. "So if you could just give me a little more time, I could get it all. I don't want to lose my house."

I wasn't supposed to make promises to a customer. My only mission here was to learn the situation and report back to Manny. He'd be the one to decide what happened with Janet's account.

But I couldn't keep my mouth shut.

"You've got half the money to bring your account current?" I asked.

Janet nodded quickly.

"Bring it to the office first thing on Monday," I said. "I'll make sure Mid-American works with you on getting caught up. I know there's something we can do to help you."

"Oh, that would be great," Janet said, and heaved a big sigh. "Want a hot dog? It's on the house."

I smiled. "No, thanks, Janet."

"I'll see you on Monday morning," she promised.

I turned away and ran smack into Nick. I hadn't realized he'd been standing behind me. I went around him back to the bleachers, empty now that the tile setting demonstration had ended, and sat down.

He came up beside me. "Does Mid-America really have a way to help her with her mortgage payments?"

"They will when I get finished talking to my boss on Monday morning," I told him.

"Damn …."

I saw that killer half-grin on his face. "What?" I asked.

"Did you ever think of becoming a cop?" he asked.

"You wouldn't like me with a gun in my hand," I told him.

"Oh, I don't know," he said softly. "I might."

Hearing Nick's mellow voice and seeing his killer-grin after dealing with yet another good person who'd gotten caught up in bad circumstances was too much. My anger spiked—and I'd been itching for this confrontation for a long time.

"Look, Nick," I said. "I want to know the truth. Did you get Katie Jo pregnant, or not?"

He just looked at me, surprised by this sudden turn in our conversation, no doubt. I couldn't blame him, but I wasn't going to back off.

"Well?" I demanded.

"Why do you want to know?" he asked.

He was avoiding the question. He'd been avoiding it for days now. The way I saw it, a lot was at stake here. Nick didn't seem to get it.

It hit me then that I should take a chance and tell him how I felt. Maybe if I took the first step, he'd follow. Maybe this whole issue would be behind us once and for all, and we'd ride off into the sunset together.

I'd like to ride off into the sunset with Nick.

"That whole thing with you and Katie Jo, I can't get past it," I said. "It's a huge wedge between us. I have to know the truth."

Nick gazed off into the parking lot as if he were thinking about it, then turned to me again.

"What happened between Katie Jo and me," he said, "is none of your business."

"It's—what?"

"It's not your concern," Nick said.

"Not my concern?" I mumbled.

So much for sunsets.

"Thanks a whole hell of a lot, Nick Travis," I told him. "I stick my feelings out there and you smack them down."

"What happened with Katie Jo has nothing to do with you and me," Nick said. "You're going to have to get over it."

"Get over it? That's your answer? *Get over it?*" I jumped off the bleachers in front of him. "I'm glad I threw your payments in the trash!"

"You—you did what?"

"I threw out your payments! Four out of the last five months!"

"I knew you threw them away," Nick told me.

"Damn right I did," I said. "I wish I'd been in the office so I could have thrown out every single one of them!"

"Do you know how much money you've cost me?" Nick demanded. "In late fees? In bank fees?"

"Yeah, I knew exactly how much I cost you," I said. "And all I can say is too bad it wasn't more!"

Nick glared at me, fury drawing his brows together.

I put my fist on my hip. "Don't stand there and act like this is all *my* fault."

Now he looked at me as if I'd lost my mind completely.

"So whose fault is it?" he wanted to know.

"Your fault."

His eyes widened. "My fault?"

"Yes," I told him. "If you'd told me the truth about Katie Jo, none of this would have happened."

"You're not making any sense at all right now," Nick said.

That was probably true.

50 Cent rapping out a song on a big set of speakers intruded on my thoughts. Over Nick's shoulder I saw a silver Lexus whip into a parking spot in front of Ryan's Electronics Warehouse.

Leonard Sullivan got out.

CHAPTER TWENTY TWO

"I've got to go," I said.

Nick looked at me as if I'd lost my mind yet another time this afternoon, and said, "You have to leave?"

"Yeah." I glanced at the electronics warehouse, then at Nick again. "Unless you're going to change your mind and tell me what happened with Katie Jo. Are you?"

"No." He shook his head. "Are you going to let it go?"

"No."

Nick didn't say anything more and neither did I. So, that was that.

I headed down the sidewalk, Leonard Sullivan in my sights, and threaded my way through the crowd and inside the store.

As I approached, I saw that Leonard had upgraded his image since the last time I'd seen him. He didn't look like the guy from Devon I'd always known. He wore nice trousers and a sport coat.

I guess this new job of his paid well.

"Hi, Leonard," I said and stopped behind him.

He turned, did a double-take and pulled off his sunglasses. I got the same look I usually got from Mid-America customers, which surprised me since Leonard didn't have an account with us.

He threw a nervous glance over the aisles, then eased closer turning his body so his back was toward the front of the store.

He shook out his shoulders trying to look cool, I guess, and forced a smile.

"Dana, what's up, girl?" he asked.

"I want to ask you the same," I said.

He gestured to the racks of CDs. "Just looking for some tunes to take partying tonight. Felderman throws an epic party, but he don't know nothing about music."

"You're going to Felderman's party?" I guess Leonard really did hang with a new crowd now. "Me, too."

He shrugged. "Everybody goes to Felderman's."

"I've been looking for you, Leonard," I said. "Your grandmother is worried about you, and so are your aunt and the rest of your family."

"Damn, girl, you just don't get it, do you?" Leonard glanced over his shoulder, then at me again, angry now.

I was angry, too.

"Leonard, I know you've had problems with your grandfather, but that's all over now. Your grandmother needs you," I said. "I'm going to have to repossess her television, and who knows if she'll be able to pay the rest of her bills."

Leonard grumbled a curse and pulled his wallet from his hip pocket. Inside was a wad of bills.

I got a sick feeling about just what sort of work Leonard's new job entailed.

He pulled out almost all of the cash and handed it to me.

"Give that to Granny," he said, and shoved his wallet into his pocket.

"Leonard, it's great that you're giving her this money, but your grandmother needs *you*," I said.

"I told you to stay away from this," Leonard said, his voice rising. "I told you."

"You haven't told me anything," I said. "We haven't seen each other since you paid off your last account in my office."

"I sent my home boy with a message," he told me. "Twice."

My stomach knotted and bounced into my throat. I gulped it down.

"At Club Vibe and the post office? That was your friend?" I asked. "He scared the crap out of me."

"Better scared than dead," he said.

A heaviness bore down on me, the kind of feeling you get when the one thing you dread the most comes true.

"You know what happened to your grandfather, don't you, Leonard?" I said.

He threw both hands up and backed off a step, shaking his head.

"I didn't have nothing to do with that," he said. "I didn't know that was going down."

"But you were there," I said, as my knees started to tremble.

Leonard didn't say anything.

"You were there," I said again. "Outside? Down the block, waiting? You recognized me when I walked into your grandfather's house."

"Stay out of this. I'm not telling you no more. You're on your own."

Leonard cut around me and disappeared.

I crammed the money into my pocket, then hurried outside.

Nick. Where was Nick? He needed to talk to Leonard.

I darted through the crowd, but didn't spot him. Apparently he hadn't hung around to try and find me, or explain things, or work anything out.

I guess I should have expected that.

I hopped in my Honda and circled the parking lot thinking I'd catch Leonard leaving so I could follow him, see where he went, maybe learn where he lived. No luck.

I pulled out onto the street and headed north, hoping I'd chosen the right direction and would spot Leonard up ahead. I didn't. I gave up and went home.

* * *

Seven Eleven met me at the door. I scooped her up and stroked her head while I stuffed the cash Leonard had given me into my underwear drawer. I'd take it to Mrs. Sullivan tomorrow; maybe by then I could think of what to tell her about Leonard.

I plopped down on my sofa ready to do some serious thinking. A lot of what I'd believed in just a few days ago had been proven wrong, which troubled me—the big thing being that good hadn't triumphed over evil.

Like Sean Griffin's murder, and Leonard Sullivan's involvement in his grandfather's death. Things with Nick definitely had not evened out.

Seven Eleven crawled onto my lap and made herself comfortable. I patted her little head and considered calling Nick, telling him what I suspected.

Leonard had been near—or at—the scene of Mr. Sullivan's murder. I hadn't wanted to face the possibility that he'd actually murdered his grandfather, but now I wasn't so sure.

He'd seen me at the house that evening and recognized me. I guess he felt we shared enough history that he wanted to protect me from the guy who'd run into me inside the house—the guy probably thought I could identify him—and to do that Leonard had sent one of his posse to warn me away from the investigation.

I suspected too that, somehow, Kirk Redmond was involved in all of this.

The afternoon Sean Griffin was murdered Slade had told me that Kirk Redmond, the building contractor, wasn't much of a building contractor. He worked a few jobs, just enough to make the place look legit, but really used the business to launder drug money.

After finally finding Leonard, seeing him in person, I knew he'd turned to dealing drugs. The new car, the nice clothes, the cash—what else could it be?

But was Leonard working with Kirk Redmond? Or was he a rival in some drug dealers' territory dispute? Had Leonard murdered Mr. Sullivan because he threatened to go to the police? Or had Redmond shot him as a warning to Leonard to get out of the business?

I didn't know. But I was sure either Leonard or Redmond had murdered Mr. Sullivan.

I had no proof, of course. All I had were names in circles written on a legal pad.

But that was enough—for me, anyway.

Again, I considered telling Nick about my suspicion. But there was a good chance he had already figured all of this out, and I didn't want to look like an idiot—or a bigger idiot than I already felt like for pouring out my heart to him in the parking lot of the Home Depot—by telling him something he already knew.

I stewed on this for a while and decided I'd think about it over the weekend and, depending how things looked on Monday, call Nick then.

I pushed the whole matter out of my mind and checked my phone messages. Mom had called.

I grabbed a soda from my fridge and returned her call. She wanted to know that I was okay since she hadn't heard from me yesterday.

You're got to love a mom like that.

She was excited about the party she and Dad were going to tonight, mum plant and all. It sounded like a yawner to me but Mom was happy and that's all I cared about.

I called Jillian. She was in a dither about her Halloween costume, Felderman's party, who'd be there, who wouldn't. After she wound down I told her I'd pick her up at 8:00.

I took a nap, and awoke rested, refreshed, my mind wiped clean of all the things had had taken up so much space there these last weeks. I had a Halloween party to go to tonight and a killer costume to wear. That would be the center of my little universe for the next several hours.

Since I was masquerading as a vixen pirate tonight, I went heavy on the makeup. I dressed in a short—very short—black skirt, fishnets, and thigh-high boots. My white blouse had elastic at the top so I pulled it down to bare both shoulders. I had to wear a strapless bra, but that was to be expected—it wasn't a special occasion without uncomfortable underwear.

I applied a temporary tattoo of a green parrot to my left shoulder, then tied a red polka dot scarf around my head, and finished off the look with a pair of huge silver earrings.

I stepped back from the mirror for a final check. Seven Eleven meowed her approval. I gave her a cuddle, got my things, and left.

Jillian needed help getting down the steps at her apartment and into my car. Her fair maiden costume was a pink sparkly ankle-length dress she could barely walk in, a wispy wrap and a pointed hat with three layers of pink veils swinging around it. Jillian really would be a damsel in distress if she needed to make an emergency run to the bathroom tonight.

This was another thing I wanted to change when I took over the world, but honestly, I didn't know how I'd manage it.

Felderman lived in the upscale area of Maywood. The party was wide-open when Jillian and I pulled up. Cars jammed the street in both directions. I parked two blocks away, and even from there we heard the music.

We left our purses in the trunk and off we went, Jillian taking baby steps in her long dress and me teetering on four inch stilettos.

The neighborhood screamed Halloween. Jack-o-lanterns sat on porches, scarecrows and witches stared out from windows. No trick-or-treaters, since Monday was Halloween. Tonight was strictly for the party crowd.

As we drew near Felderman's big two story house, we saw people on his lawn laughing, drinking, talking too loud. Every window in the house was lit. The front door stood open. People drifted in and out.

Everybody was in costume—everything imaginable, to every degree of taste. I spotted a cowboy, a showgirl, and a sumo wrestler that I could have gone my whole life without seeing. Jillian and I found friends right away. We chatted about each other's costumes, waved and yelled to people as we made our way inside.

The place was packed. We squeezed toward the rear of the house in the direction of the bar, where the biggest crowd congregated. French doors opened to the patio. Outside, the deejay had set up at the edge of a makeshift dance floor that was killing Felderman's grass.

"Hey, Dana," someone called.

Jarrod Parker appeared at my elbow.

Stunned, I asked, "What are you doing here?"

He shrugged. "Everybody comes to Felderman's party. Want a drink?"

I wish I could say I liked Jarrod better since Nick told me this afternoon that he had no criminal record and no involvement in Mr. Sullivan or Sean Griffin's murders. There was still something weird about the guy.

But at least I didn't have to be afraid of Jarrod. He was harmless. And as long as I couldn't seem to get rid of him, he might as well do something for me.

"Get me a beer, will you?" I asked, and he headed toward the kegs.

Jillian and I mingled. Jarrod fought his way back to me with a plastic cup of beer. I grabbed it and we headed for the nearest exit, the French doors.

The music pounded. The crowd was close. I sipped my beer feeling that everything was right in my little world.

I spotted a couple of friends at the corner of the house, so Jillian and I worked our way toward them. Somehow, Jarrod ended up at my side again, and I was ready to tell him to get lost when Jillian caught my arm and spun me around. She pointed toward the dance floor.

"Are those your parents?" she asked.

The crowd around the dance floor had broken back and was clapping along with a solitary couple at center stage—my parents, all right.

Mom had given herself big hair and had on a dress I remembered from my junior high graduation. Dad wore his powder blue leisure suit. They were dancing the bump to "Brick House."

Jarrod elbowed me. "Cool costumes."

"Yeah, my folks are way cool," I said. And they were.

We circled the house, went through the gate in the wooden fence that enclosed the backyard, and found an open spot on the front lawn. For some reason, Jarrod came, too.

I sipped my beer while people flowed around us drinking, talking, gathering in knots and moving on again. Jarrod blabbed on about something I wasn't paying attention to.

When I finished my beer, Jarrod offered to get me another. I turned to answer him, but my gaze caught the profile of a face in a group of men across the lawn.

I stood there for a minute watching him, thinking, trying to place him.

Then I remembered.

He was the man I'd seen in Mr. Sullivan's living room.

CHAPTER TWENTY THREE

My heart beat faster. My knees felt wobbly.

It was definitely the man I'd seen at the Sullivan house. The man who'd knocked me down. No doubt about it.

I eased my way across the yard and inserted myself into a cluster of people a little closer to him. He was tall, six-three easily, slender, blond. Good looking.

His costume was a pinstripe suit reminiscent of the '20s, complete with a fedora. He looked like an old school gangster, but a classy one. If my suspicion was correct, his choice of costume wasn't coincidental.

He stood in profile so I caught just the side of his face, the tip of his nose, his cheekbone, his chin. Just like at Mr. Sullivan's house. The lighting here wasn't great, same as at Mr. Sullivan's, but it was good enough for me to know this was the man, and I was sure he was Kirk Redmond, the final name I'd entered in the circles on my legal pad. The name that completed my dot-to-dot puzzle and formed a complete picture. The picture of a murderer.

My stomach did an oh-my-God heave, and I wished I could get a do-over on my decision not to call Nick with my suspicion.

My thoughts raced. Why was Redmond here? Maybe he was just a party guest. Everybody came to Felderman's party.

Or was he here because of me?

But how would he have known I'd be here? True, it wasn't exactly a secret. He might have followed me, a thought that made my skin crawl, or maybe—

Leonard. I'd told Leonard I was coming to the party when I'd seen him this afternoon at Ryan's Electronics Warehouse. He must have told Redmond.

I realized then that I hadn't seen Leonard here tonight, even though he'd said he was coming.

I started to feel sick. Seemed Leonard and Redmond were in business together, after all.

It hit me that since I'd spotted Redmond, he might spot me, too. He knew who I was, especially since I'd been thoughtful enough to telephone his place of business, identify myself, report that I knew he'd been at Mr. Sullivan's house—no wonder he saw me as a threat—and even provided him with my contact info.

I felt relatively safe in the big party crowd. Still, I had to do something.

If I called the cops they'd come with sirens blaring and would surely incite a panic. I'd seen several under-age kids drinking beer inside the house, and at least two people who weren't here with their spouses; the scent of something illegal floated in the air.

Somebody might get trampled. Kirk Redmond could easily slip away in the confusion.

I'd call Nick. But how to get in touch with him?

My cell phone was locked up safe and sound in the trunk of my car two blocks down the street. My pepper spray was there, too. Slade would be so disappointed in me.

My herding instinct—the one that drove women to the restroom in packs—was doing double duty right now, so no way was I leaving the safety of the party.

Jillian had found some friends and Jarrod had vanished in a puff of smoke, so I headed into the house. I climbed the staircase to the second floor and opened the first bedroom on my right. Two people had gotten to this room before me and were heavily involved in what I suppose in some cultures passed for love making. I slammed the door and continued down the hallway.

I found the master bedroom, situated at the front of the house. It was unoccupied. I peered out the window as I picked up the telephone beside the bed, and called the police.

I was transferred a few times, put on hold, and while I waited I realized that if Redmond decided to leave the party, he could disappear and who knew when he'd surface again? If, as I suspected, he knew I could identify him and tie him to Mr. Sullivan's murder, he might head for safer climes.

I tapped my stiletto heel against Felderman's gray carpet and finally somebody picked up. I told the guy who I was, explained the situation as best I could, and asked him to forward my message to Nick immediately.

I hung up and glanced out the window again. Redmond wasn't

standing with the same group of people. No way was I going to let him get away. I hurried downstairs.

I eased through the crowd wearing a fake smile, trying to look for him without being obvious about it. I got jostled, had beer spilled on my arm and my butt grabbed, but I didn't see him.

In the backyard the dance floor was packed. I made my way around to the side of the house and walked through the wooden gate.

A hand closed around my arm pulling me up short. I gasped and glanced over my shoulder.

Kirk Redmond.

His face was shadowed by the fedora he wore. He leaned down and I felt his breath against my cheek.

"Dana Mackenzie," he whispered.

"Kirk Redmond," I said, finding strength from somewhere to make my lips move.

"Let's you and me go for a little walk," he said.

I dug my stiletto heels into the ground and said, "I don't think so."

Redmond pulled a pistol from the pocket of his pinstripe jacket just far enough that I could see it in his hand.

"Want to change your answer, Dana?" he asked.

A chill went down my spine. I shook my head and said, "I'll stay here."

Redmond stretched his chin up, took a deep breath, and eased closer until his body touched mine. He leaned down and spoke softly into my ear.

"Then how about I go into the backyard and ask your mother to go with me?"

I nearly fainted.

Redmond jerked my arm. "What's it going to be, Dana? You or your mom?"

How could he have found out about my mom? How did he know who she was?

Then a really sick feeling swept over me. I'd given him my folks' phone number so my dad could talk to him about painting the Sullivan house. Redmond had found out where they lived—no big trick with the Internet these days—checked them out, had them followed, and was probably delighted to realize they were headed to Felderman's party.

"I'll go with you," I said.

He kept his left hand locked around my upper arm and his right hand in his pocket with the gun. We skirted the edge of Felderman's lawn, bypassing the other party-goers, and headed down the sidewalk.

I glanced over my shoulder. No sign of Jillian, my best friend. All the other people I knew were laughing, drinking, and partying hearty. Even that idiot Jarrod Parker was nowhere to be seen, the one time I needed him.

I had the sickening feeling this was the last party I'd ever go to.

Redmond pulled me between two parked cars and across the street. We stepped up onto the sidewalk on the other side and kept walking. I guessed he was taking me to his car and it was parked a good ways from the party, as was mine. Only mine was in the opposite direction.

At this point I figured I was a goner. I was no match for Redmond's strength. He had a gun. I doubted he had any reservations about using it—again—so I decided I may as well satisfy my own curiosity about everything that had gone down.

"Did Belinda pick out that costume for you?" I asked.

Redmond's steps faltered. He glared down at me but kept walking, giving me my answer.

"You were the contractor on the patio at her house. That's how you met, right?" I said.

Home improvements financed by Mid-America's second mortgage. Home improvements that eventually cost Sean Griffin his life.

"You do good work. I was at the house. I saw what you'd done." I said. "I guess the contracting business doesn't pay as well as drug dealing, though."

We passed under a street lamp and the yellow light illuminated us for a few seconds. I watched the houses we passed hoping to see someone at a window or in their yard. Nothing.

"I guess Belinda needed your drug money," I said. "That gambling habit of hers must be a killer."

I'd seen the glazed over look in Belinda's eyes the day I'd run into her at the Indian casino. She wasn't there for the fun of it, as Leona and the other ladies were. Belinda was in deep—which explained why she had all those credit cards, why they were all maxed out, why Sean had found their savings account empty, their bills past due, and their home teetering on foreclosure.

"Belinda met Leonard at the casino," I said. "She's the one who put him in touch with you, right?"

Redmond still didn't answer.

"Nice of you to burn down her house for her. I guess it took care of a lot of her problems. She's all yours now, with Sean out of the way." I looked up at Redmond. "Did you really have to kill him?"

He finally spoke. I guess he saw no reason not to, considering he planned to kill me shortly.

"If he'd butted out, that wouldn't have happened," Redmond said.

"He threatened to take her kids."

"I guess he was a complication you didn't need," I said.

"So are you." Redmond uttered a gruff laugh. "Leonard said he had you under control. But then Belinda saw you at the casino with Leonard's aunt. You made the connection. You got greedy. You tried to blackmail me."

"Blackmail?"

"Leonard didn't know you as well as he thought," Redmond said.

"I wasn't trying to blackmail you. I just wanted you to paint the Sullivan house."

"Yeah, sure."

We stopped beside a black BMW parked at the curb and Redmond opened the passenger side door.

No way was I getting into that car.

"Do you really think killing me is going to solve another problem?" I asked, just for something to say, just to give myself a few more seconds to think.

Redmond crowded me against the car. "Get in."

My heart pounded in my chest. I had to do something. Anything. I wasn't going willingly to my death.

I feigned a move toward the car, raised my knee and drove my four-inch stiletto heel into Redmond's ankle. It went in deep, thanks to my firm thigh muscles made possible by my diligent jogging.

He howled. I jerked away, ducked under his arm and took off down the sidewalk.

I wanted to head back to the party, to the crowd, to security, but that direction was a straight line down the street, an easy shot for Redmond to make with that pistol of his. I ran the other way.

I cut across the lawn at the corner house, onto another street. Surely someone would be outside. Someone leaving their house, or arriving home. Somebody walking their dog. Somebody doing *something*.

I saw no one.

My initial surge of adrenaline kept me going, but running in thigh-high boots and a strapless bra wasn't the best way to go. Should I bang on a door? Hide in shrubbery? Try to climb a fence into someone's backyard?

I got tackled from behind. A full body blow. I fell face down onto the grass, Redmond on top of me.

He scrambled to his feet pulling me up with him, as he fumbled with his pocket, going for his gun.

Strapless bra or not, I went wild. I kicked, punched, clawed, screamed. I wasn't going down without a fight, without some of

Redmond's DNA under my fingernails.

Apparently, he was used to a little tamer type of woman because I got away from him. Headlights beamed down the street. I ran toward them waving my arms and screaming.

Redmond caught me again as I reached the sidewalk. I elbowed his ribs. He caught a fistful of my hair and pulled his pistol from his pocket.

I'd be dead in seconds. My life flashed before my eyes.

A white light covered me. It drew nearer growing more intense, blinding me.

Were the angels coming for me?

If so, they'd arrived in a Chevy Camaro.

The car jumped the curb, high-beams glaring, and skidded to a stop a few feet from us. Nick jumped out, pistol drawn.

"Freeze! Police!"

Redmond hung there for another second or two, holding my hair, holding the pistol. Nick stood behind his open car door, arm extended, aiming his weapon directly at Redmond.

"Put the gun down," Nick shouted. "Put it down!"

Redmond let me go. He tossed the pistol away.

"Get down on the ground," Nick told him.

Redmond cursed, but stretched out on the grass, arms and legs spread.

I started to shake. I touched my hair. It was in a million tangles. My cute little red polka dot pirate scarf was gone. I was missing an earring. I had grass stains on my blouse and big runs in my fishnets.

"You bastard!" I shouted.

I kicked Kirk Redmond in the ribs.

CHAPTER TWENTY FOUR

I don't usually jog on Sundays but today I made an exception. The afternoon was great—perfect Southern California weather. Three Days Grace blasted in my ears soothing me in a strange way. And I needed to be soothed.

Aside from a few scrapes and bruises, I had no outward signs of my ordeal at Felderman's party last night. The other injuries I'd sustained were on the inside. Thankfully, they were all on the mend. It was just a matter of time.

I circled my complex a final time and returned to the stairs leading to my apartment. Nick appeared on the step beside me. I was glad to see him.

I pulled out my ear buds and smiled. He smiled back.

"I was waiting for you," he said, and nodded toward my apartment.

"Did you bring chocolate?" I asked, peering around him.

"No. Just me."

For some reason, that sounded better than chocolate.

"Want to come upstairs?" I asked.

We got up, but a honking horn drew our attention. A black Coupe de Ville cruised to a stop in front of us. The top was down. Inside were Leona Wiley, Ruby, Helen and Dora. On the passenger side of the front seat sat Gladys Sullivan. All of them were dressed in their finest, clutching handbags on their laps.

Slade was behind the wheel.

"Hi, ladies," I greeted as Nick and I walked over. "What are you up to?"

"Road trip!" Ruby declared.

"We're hitting the highway," Helen said.

"Going to Vegas!" Dora shouted.

I looked at Slade. He just shrugged and said, "It's cool, babe."

Then I remembered something. I tore up the stairs, got the money Leonard had given me yesterday, and went back to the car. I passed it to Mrs. Sullivan.

"From Leonard," I said.

"Is he all right?" she asked. "I've been so worried."

I glanced at Nick, then said, "Leonard's in a little trouble, but he wanted you to have this money. I'm sure he'll call you as soon as he can."

"Thank you, honey," Mrs. Sullivan said.

"Looks like Glady's mojo is working already," Dora declared, and the other ladies laughed.

Mrs. Sullivan peeled off several of the bills and passed them back to me. "Put this on our account, will you?"

"Sure," I said, slipping the money into my pocket.

I heaved a mental sigh, glad that Mrs. Sullivan could keep her Sony television and watch her stories to her heart's content.

Slade leaned toward me. "Gladys isn't going to need mojo in Vegas. She's got this car and it's worth a nice chunk of change."

My eyebrows did a this-thing? bob.

"I know a classic car collector who wants to see it. He's willing to lay down about hundred grand for it," Slade said.

All I could do was smile.

"Well, you kids have fun," I said.

The ladies waved as Slade drove away.

Nick and I stood there watching until they disappeared, then we went upstairs and into my apartment.

Seven Eleven rubbed against Nick's legs, then trotted into the kitchen and hung out by her bowl. He poured dry food for her, then got two beers from the fridge and passed one to me.

"I heard your folks were the hit of the party," Nick said.

"They're really cool parents," I said. But if Mom and Dad intended to be part of the party scene from now on, I was definitely taking both of them shopping.

Nick leaned against the counter. "Leonard Sullivan was picked up."

"Did he tell you anything?" I asked.

"He confessed to being a drug dealer in Redmond's organization," he said.

"Please tell me Leonard didn't mean for Mr. Sullivan to get killed," I said.

"His story is that his grandfather suspected what he was doing, threatened to go to the police and expose Redmond, thinking it would keep Leonard out of trouble," Nick said. "When Leonard told Redmond, the two of them went to Sullivan's house. Leonard thought Redmond was just going put some fear in him. He didn't know he intended to kill him."

"Do you believe him?" I asked.

"I believe him," Nick said, which made me feel a little better.

"How about Belinda?" I asked.

"Picked her up, too. She cracked, confessed to her affair with Redmond and to conspiring with him to torch her own house," Nick said. "She claimed it was because of her addiction to gambling and the bills she'd piled up."

"Did she know Redmond intended to kill Sean?" I asked.

Nick paused. "She says she didn't, but I'm not so sure."

I was sure.

"What about their children?" I asked.

"Sean's mom has them," he said.

I shook my head. "I knew there was something weird about Belinda but I never figured she'd do something like this. Sure, having an affair, getting into debt, spending all of Sean's money is something I can understand—not agree with, of course, but understand," I said. "But having her boyfriend burn down her house? Having Sean killed?"

"She wanted him out of her life. He threatened to take her kids away," Nick said. "Gambling. It takes over, like drugs or booze."

"Yeah," I said, "but what about love?"

"Are you talking about us?" Nick asked.

I almost choked on my beer. "Us?"

"Yes, Dana," he said, and set his beer on the counter. "Us."

"There is no *us*," I said.

"Because of what happened with Katie Jo and me back in high school?" he asked.

"Exactly," I told him.

Nick looked at me for a few seconds, and said, "Maybe there was more to the story than you knew."

"Like what?"

"Maybe it wasn't me who got her pregnant," Nick said. "Maybe I was covering for someone else."

"Are you saying that's what happened?" I asked.

Nick shook his head. "I'm simply asking if you'd ever considered either of those things."

"Well, no," I admitted.

Nick took the beer bottle from my hand and set it on the counter.

"Doesn't it reassure you to know that I'm good at keeping secrets?" he asked.

"Why should it?" I asked.

Nick put his hands on my shoulders and gave me one of his infamous grins.

"Because if I get you pregnant," he said. "you won't have to worry about me telling anyone."

My insides fluttered. "That won't happen."

"Are you sure about that?" Nick lowered his head until his lips fanned my cheek. "I'm willing to prove it to you."

My knees nearly gave out. He slid his arm around me. All I could focus on was Nick and how close he was, how good he smelled.

"Are you going to forget about Katie Jo and me?" Nick murmured against my neck.

"No," I said, though I was having trouble focusing. "Are you going to tell me the truth about you two?"

"No," Nick said.

I put my hand on his chest and leaned back a little.

"I'm telling you, Nick, nothing will ever go on between us until I know what happened with you and Katie Jo," I said.

"We'll see about that," he whispered.

Nick smiled and I started to melt. I couldn't help it. He'd had that effect on me since high school.

He pulled me close. It felt good, really good. Then he kissed me.

Ahh ... so this is what it's like to own the world.

THE END

Dear Reader,

Thanks for giving the Fatal Debt a try! I hope you'll look for Fatal Luck, the next installment in the Dana Mackenzie series.

If you enjoyed this book, you'll probably also like my Haley Randolph mystery series available from Kensington Books in hardcover, paperback, and ebook formats. Haley is an amateur sleuth whose passion for designer handbags leads to murder.

More information is available at www.DorothyHowellNovels.com and at my Dorothy Howell Novels fan page on Facebook. You can follow me on Twitter @DHowellNovels.

If you're a romance reader, I also write historical fiction under the pen name Judith Stacy. You're invited to check out www.JudithStacy.com.

Happy reading!
Dorothy

BOOKS BY DOROTHY HOWELL

The Haley Randolph Mystery Series
Handbags and Homicide
Purses and Poison
Shoulder Bags and Shootings
Clutches and Curses
Tote Bags and Toe Tags
Evening Bags and Executions
Beach Bags and Burglaries

The Dana Mackenzie Mystery Series
Fatal Debt
Fatal Luck

ABOUT THE AUTHOR

Dorothy Howell is the author of 35 novels. She's written for three major New York publishing houses. Her books have been translated into a dozen languages, with sales approaching 4 million copies worldwide.

Dorothy currently writes for two publishing houses, in two genres, under two names.

HANDBAGS AND HOMICIDE launched her hardcover mystery series from Kensington Publishing. Six more novels have followed, along with two novellas. The Haley Randolph series has sold in the U.K., France, Thailand, and Poland, and is available in Large Print and e-book editions.

FATAL DEBT, Dorothy's first stand-alone mystery which introduces amateur sleuth Dana Mackenzie, is also available.

Dorothy also writes historical romance novels under the pen name Judith Stacy. Her titles include Harlequin Historical's Top Seller of the Year, a No.1 on the Barnes & Noble historical list, and a RITA Award Finalist. Her books are available in paperback, Large Print, and e-book formats. More information is available at www.JudithStacy.com.

Dorothy got the idea for the Haley Randolph mystery series set in the world of retail when her daughter, a college student, took a part-time job in a department store. After hearing the stories about problems with management, customers, and co-workers, Dorothy was reminded of how brutal a retail job can be. So brutal, in fact, that she decided, "This would make a great book!"

After getting the inside story from her daughter, and a tour of the store's stock room, the character of Haley Randolph was born. She's edgy, sassy, and like many of us, she just can't seem to catch a break.

The "handbag" aspect of the mystery series comes from Dorothy's passion for designer purses. Her heart actually beats faster in the presence of beautiful purses, and once, she almost licked the display window at a Louis Vuitton store.

Dorothy is a member of Sisters in Crime, Mystery Writers of America, and Romance Writers of America. She's a requested speaker at writing, civic, and women's organizations, and has appeared on television and radio promoting her work.

Dorothy lives in Southern California. She's eternally grateful for the love and support of family and friends, her hard working agent and publisher, and her extreme good fortune.

Connect with Dorothy Here:
www.DorothyHowellNovels.com
www.JudithStacy.com
www.Facebook.com
twitter.com@DHowellNovels

Made in the USA
Middletown, DE
23 October 2014